GET FLUFFY

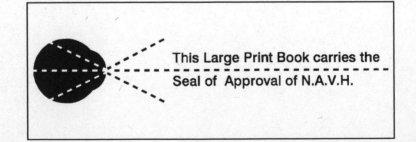

This Large Print Book carries the
Seal of Approval of N.A.V.H.

GET FLUFFY

SPARKLE ABBEY

THORNDIKE PRESS
A part of Gale, Cengage Learning

Detroit • New York • San Francisco • New Haven, Conn • Waterville, Maine • London

GALE
CENGAGE Learning·

Copyright © 2012 by Anita Carter and Mary Lee Woods, writing as Sparkle Abbey.
Thorndike Press, a part of Gale, Cengage Learning.

Thorndike Press® Large Print Clean Reads.
The text of this Large Print edition is unabridged.
Other aspects of the book may vary from the original edition.
Set in 16 pt. Plantin.

LIBRARY OF CONGRESS CATALOGING-IN-PUBLICATION DATA

Abbey, Sparkle.
  Get fluffy / by Sparkle Abbey.
    pages ; cm. — (Thorndike Press large print clean reads)
    ISBN 978-1-4104-5277-1 (hardcover) — ISBN 1-4104-5277-8 (hardcover) 1.
Laguna Beach (Calif.)—Fiction. 2. Dogs—Fiction. 3. Murder—Fiction. 4. Large
type books. I. Title.
  PS3601.B359G48 2012b
  813'.6—dc23   2012032381

Published in 2012 by arrangement with BelleBooks, Inc.

Printed in the United States of America
1 2 3 4 5 6 7 16 15 14 13 12

This book is dedicated to Team Sparkle Abbey. An amazing group of friends and family, who enthusiastically attend book signings, handout bookmarks, master our website and ask perfect strangers what they're reading. Thank-you will never be enough.

CHAPTER ONE

I am nothing like my cousin, Caro, the "pet shrink."

She's a redhead, I'm a brunette. She's kept her Texas twang, I busted my butt to lose mine. (Except when I'm honked off, then my southern drawl can strike like a Gulf coast hurricane.) She's calm and direct. I'm equally direct. As for calm, I have to admit, sometimes my emotions tend to overrule my better judgment.

So who would have thought I'd end up in the middle of a Laguna Beach murder investigation, just like Caro?

From my very first breath, Mama had groomed me to be Miss America, just like her and her sister, Katherine. Or a Dallas Cowboy Cheerleader, which in Texas was the more prestigious of the two. By my twenty-first birthday, I'd gathered ten first-place pageant crowns like Fourth of July parade candy. That's when my beauty queen career had been dethroned in public scandal.

Everyone believed she "encouraged" a male judge to cast his vote for me. As for what I thought, well, no daughter wants to believe her mama is a hustler. To this day, Mama still won't talk about *The Incident* above a whisper.

With the battle for the top crown over, I'd traded in my tiaras, sashes and hair spray for Swarovski crystal collars, cashmere dog sweaters and botanical flea dip. I left Texas and moved to Laguna Beach, California, a community known for its art, wealth and love of dogs. I opened Bow Wow Boutique and catered to the canine who had everything.

I loved Laguna. Loved running my own business. I even loved the quirky folks whose lives revolved around their pooches. But sometimes I longed for Texas — wide open spaces, cowboy boots and big-big hair. Who wouldn't?

It was mid-October. The tourists had packed up and headed home. The locals ventured out of their gated communities to enjoy all the beachside town had to offer. Most importantly, there was available parking downtown. At least until next May.

The annual Fur Ball had finally arrived —

a community event to raise money for the Laguna Beach Animal Rescue League. The balmy weather was perfect for an outdoor fundraiser.

As always at these shindigs, the humans coughed up large chunks of dough for a worthy cause. Breezy air kisses and alcohol flowed freely, while we all pretended to be best friends. Trust me, we were one society catfight away from a hell of an entertaining evening.

I looked down at Missy, my English Bulldog, who waited patiently at my feet. Her crystal-studded tiara sat lopsided on the top of her head, and a small puddle of drool had collected between her paws.

I straightened her crown and whispered, "We're up, girl. Let's show them what we've got."

With our heads held high, Missy and I strutted our stuff down the red carpet. The pup-a-razzi cameras flashed, and the crowd cheered. One reporter asked who'd made my strapless leather gown (Michael Kors) and another wanted to know how Missy had won her tiara (she'd placed first in Laguna Beach's Ugliest Bulldog contest last year).

Once we reached the end of the walkway, I leaned down to dab the drool from Missy's chin. "You did great." I kissed the top of her head. "Let's go find our friends."

Missy gave my hand a slobbery kiss, and then we made our way into the main event. Under an extravagant white tent and glittering lights, two hundred wealthy dog lovers and their four-legged friends paraded around in designer rags, both human and canine dripped with diamonds.

I quickly spotted Kimber Shores and her pug Noodles making their way in our direction. Kimber oozed understated glamour in her mauve jumpsuit. She'd definitely make Laguna's Best-Dressed List.

"Mel, I'm so glad I found you," she declared.

As we air kissed, the low-cut back of her outfit offered a glimpse of her many tattoos.

"Noodles looks amazing," she continued in her melodious voice. "I'm so glad you talked me out of the velvet jacket."

Kimber and her pug had stopped by the shop earlier. Noodles had been in desperate need of a wardrobe update. I'd managed to wrangle him out of his Hugh Hefner smoking jacket and into a modest white tux and tails. Noodles sat in front of Missy, his marble eyes watching the slobber slide down the corners of her mouth.

I smiled affectionately. "He really isn't a velvet kinda guy. I love the top hat. Nice choice."

Out of the corner of my eye I could see Grey Donovan, my fiancé of two years, heading in our direction. Kimber must have noticed, too; she immediately looked uncomfortable.

To the outside world, Grey's and my relationship was seen as a tad unorthodox. We were the on-again, off-again type. Presently, we were "on."

"Ah, I see you're not alone. Anyway, I just wanted to say thanks." She grabbed my hand and squeezed.

"You're welcome. Stop by Bow Wow when you get a chance. I have the perfect sweater-vest for Noodles."

Kimber and her pug disappeared into the crowd just as Grey arrived.

"Caro and Diana organized a great event." He handed me a glass of pinot noir. He looked amazing in his black tux. But then, he always looked good.

Missy sniffed his pant leg, double-checking he hadn't stepped out on her. He bent down and gave her some love. She snorted happily, lapping up Grey's affection. I knew exactly how she felt.

I took a sip of wine, appreciating the black-pepper finish. I snagged us each a tomato and goat cheese tart from a passing waiter (he was out of pigs-in-a-blanket, Missy's favorite).

"I hate to break it to you, but it's the Dallas upbringing. Every society girl knows how to throw a successful charity fundraiser by her eighteenth birthday." I took a bite of the tart and sighed. Delicious. "But you're right. It's a fabulous evening."

Grey, an undercover FBI agent, worked white-collar crime — mostly art theft. He could be gone for two days or two months without a whisper of his well-being. I never knew if he was sipping espresso in Paris or being held hostage in a deserted warehouse in East LA.

His decision to keep me completely in the dark of his activities — his way of protecting me — had finally pushed me to the breaking point. I'd realized if I had trouble *dating* Grey, our marriage could end up a disaster. So I'd called off the wedding (two months before the big day), causing a swirl of rumors and speculation.

I swear, I'd tried to return the six-carat sapphire engagement ring that had belonged to his great-grandmother, but Grey had refused to accept it. He believed we could work it out. I really wanted him to be right.

"To Caro and Diana. May the evening continue to be a howling success." Grey

12

Several years ago I began working as a volunteer at a cancer-treatment facility in New York City. The children and teenage patients scorned the sentimental books and melodramatic movies they had seen about people who were living with cancer. Many of them asked me to write about how it really is for families when a child has cancer. This novel is based on our experiences—although the characters and Mercy Hospital itself are drawn from my imagination.

For allowing me to share with them the task of living with cancer I am grateful to Barbara Balzarano, Lauren Goldman, Mindy Laks, Larry Rosado, Steven Hedinger, Woogie Cook, Tammy Kuhar, Lauren Lacy, Barbara Reilly, Markie Rodemacher, Marie Elena Di Fabio, Michelle Spence, Ajay Chitkara, Justin Allen, Joe Nicholino, Michael Martin, Stanley Lane and John Bria.

I hope I have kept our promise.

"That which was a trial to you in my flesh
ye despised not nor rejected;
but ye received me."

Galatians 4:14

Part One

One

"Where is Becky Maitland?" Coach Hawkins shouted.

The locker room was noisy. The girls' varsity basketball team was getting dressed for the afternoon game against Englishtown.

Theo Maitland stood on the bench in front of her locker and scanned the room for her twin.

"Becky?" the coach asked.

"No, Coach, I'm Theo. Becky'll be along any minute. We had a math quiz, she got held up." Theo jumped down, stripped off her jeans and hurled them into the locker. Becky was cutting it too close. Theo was running out of excuses. Not that Coach Hawkins was fooled. Lately Becky had been leaning all over Jay in the halls and outside the Senior lunchroom. As though he were the first boy she had ever gone with!

To make the situation worse Theo found Jay as appealing as cold fried eggs. She and Becky had never been so wide apart about any person as they were about Jay. Theo recoiled at Becky's starting sentences "Jay says . . ."

Rusty Wheeler sat down on the bench next to Theo. "That Englishtown team better pray for a miracle, all they got is a couple puny girls who couldn't jump over a toadstool in a rainstorm."

"Is Becky Maitland in here?"

Farther down the bench Carmela Winters stood up. "No, Coach, but I'm all ready to start." Carmela turned to Theo. "Where is Becky harin' off to when we have a big game? It must be hard for Jay to have a girl like the superstar Becky Maitland around, she gets her name on the sports page more than he does."

Theo was determined not to let the birdlike creature frazzle her. Vicious and nervous underneath a cloud of dark frizzed hair, Carmela bounced around on the perimeter of Theo and Becky's friends, scattering jealous remarks the way a chicken farmer scatters grain.

Rusty put an arm around Carmela's shoulders. "What are we going to do with you, Carmela? If you don't snag yourself a boyfriend soon, you goin' to hate us all to *death*."

"Becky Maitland! Last call!"

[4]

Theo cursed Jay under her breath.

"Thanks for corking Carmela, Rusty."

"She's never had a boy care enough for her to give a damn if she changed into a cabbage overnight."

"I know, but Becky's been carrying *on* lately," Theo admitted. "She's been going with Jay over a year now, and she acts goofy, my own sister, *wimpy.*"

"Maybe it's true love." Rusty sighed. "Maybe they'll get married."

"When pigs whistle," Theo said.

One of the starting forwards, Janice Baker, sat next to Theo. "Coach says if Becky's late one more time she's starting Carmela at center."

"Don't tell me, tell Becky," Theo snapped. Theo knew the coach held her as much responsible as Becky. Part of being twins was being treated as though they were interchangeable.

"Think Becky could really be losing her drive?" Rusty asked.

"When pigs whistle." Theo laughed.

Rusty whistled "Who's Afraid of the Big Bad Wolf?"

"Becky's in top shape, she's as good as ever," Theo insisted. "She's got more discipline than anyone on the team.

"When we were little Becky decided to do a backward flip dive as a surprise for Dad's birthday. The swimming teacher at the Club said we weren't near a dive of that difficulty, which was enough to sideline me, but not old Becky. She marched herself down to the pool at seven every morning and dove into that freezing water. Even the teacher admitted she had more guts than a kid twice her age." Theo laced her sneaker more tightly. "Make no mistake, Becky is the best."

Underneath her words Theo knew she was saying they were both the best. Theo recalled Becky's dive so vividly because of the fierce jealousy she had felt the day Becky dove for their father. She had decided then that whatever Becky did, she would do. Theo played basketball because Becky loved basketball. In order to equal Becky Theo had to practice twice as hard. After the summer of the dive Theo had decided that Becky was the better athlete. Theo depended on Becky's single-mindedness, her determination to work out every day, to goad herself into the necessary discipline to win. Becky's slacking off frightened Theo because she lacked the skill and the drive to win without her twin.

"I got to get my tail in gear. Coach freaks when we're late," Becky said.

"You're logging more practice time this fall than I am," Jay complained.

She giggled and kissed his neck, on her favorite spot just below his ear. "You going to watch the game with Mom and the boys?"

"No need to. I know you'll win. You always do. You could beat them if you spotted them one leg."

"Even the great Becky Maitland can't run on one leg." Becky kissed his cheek. "Coming over to-night?"

Jay shook his head. "My mom saw my chem test. 'No extracurricular activities, you must discipline yourself,' " he mocked. " 'You must remember your goal is college.' "

"Seems like all we hear about these days is college."

"We'll have the whole weekend," Jay told her. "Dad got us a map so we won't get lost on Columbine."

"Theo and Freddy know the route cold; they camped there last summer."

"Going with them was a lousy idea. The whole point was for us to be alone for the weekend."

"Well, Theo said she wanted to come, what could I tell her? Anyway she and Freddy can help you with your chem while we are sitting around the campfire—" Becky broke off. Whenever Jay got annoyed she jollied him out of it by slipping sexual innuendos into their conversation. She pouted and her voice became squeaky and coy. She could see Theo's face, impatient with Becky's appearing mindless and giddy.

"I solved the chem problem, my bunky basketball player. I have Robert Pincus's notes."

"Having his notes is like having Farrah Fawcett's T-shirt. Nothin' but a piece of cotton unless you supply the goodies to go inside—get my drift?" She tapped Jay's chest lightly. "Kiss me for luck. Sometimes I wish everybody didn't count on me and Theo so much."

"Get off it, Becky. No one cares if the girls' varsity wins, loses, or forfeits."

Becky shuddered at Jay's harsh tone. More every day she counted on him. From the day he arrived in Maplewood, golden, with a gelid assurance that still made her dizzy, she wanted him. Having known him for two years, she thought she was an expert at what buttons to push to please Jay. She knew he could leave her as easily as he had taken up with her.

Jay ran his fingertips along the inside of her forearm. "If you weren't playing this afternoon we could have my house to ourselves."

"I wouldn't desert the team," Becky said without much conviction. "Besides, Theo would kill me."

They both turned at the sound of Rusty shouting Becky's name.

"It's hell hanging out with a star," Jay said. Becky laughed as though it were a swell joke. He watched her walk to the gym, that special loping stride, her books balanced lightly against her hip. He felt such pride in her. Even his father, who had last week criticized the Pope for being too Catholic, had only praise for Becky. "Girl's got a head on her shoulders, not like those you went with in the city. She's neat and tidy, polite too, and a good-looker; girl like Becky will fit in anywhere."

No doubt about it, this time Jay had found himself an A-plus girl.

The gym was crowded. Before the publicity surrounding the Maitland girls the varsity basketball team had had no cheering section. The canny editor of the *Maplewood Herald* had used stories about the twins to stem the public grousing about the younger generation's obsession with dope. He understood that the town's subscribers didn't want to read more bad news. They could hear the world's mistakes on the TV news. He told his staff, "People pay through the nose to live in a town like Maplewood for a quiet, unexciting life."

So the *Herald* ran seasonal features—the twins diving into the Community pool, holding snow shovels over their shoulders like muskets, raking leaves at the Old Age Home, leading a Teen Drive for recycling aluminum cans.

Becky enjoyed the newspaper stories. They gave her assurance that raking leaves and collecting cans were important and that she was a good person to be doing such things. She liked being recognized around town. To Theo it was a chance to clown. She delighted in shocking the reporters with wild tales about throwing garbage out of car windows. It was a double security to know that they didn't believe her.

"Some swell town, so tranquil, so well ordered that they depend on my kiddoes for front-page razzle."

Dick Maitland saved their clippings and posed proudly alongside his daughters.

Becky stripped off her red leg warmers. She slicked her hair behind her ears and did a few knee bends. The locker room was deserted; she could hear the girls taking their practice shots. She wished Jay would come to the games and shout her name when she scored a basket.

She ran out to the gym floor and joined the line of girls shaking hands with the Englishtown team.

"Hey Becky!" she heard as the ball swished through the net.

She turned and waved to her mother and two brothers, sitting in the bleachers opposite center court.

"No time, Mickey," she called to her brother. She heard the two short whistle blasts and ran with her teammates to Coach Hawkins. Becky felt her confidence growing. Englishtown's center was stocky, feisty, but she had no power in her legs. Becky could outjump her easily. The coach had noticed the Englishtown center too.

"Just play your steady game, Becky, let her foul you, she can't touch your shooting accuracy, she's so short she'll always be behind you going downcourt."

All the girls laughed, squeezed hands, and Becky went to the center circle. A cheer went up from the Maplewood side of the gym.

"Mom, how come Becky's playing and Theo isn't?" Robin asked.

"Because, jerk, Theo's a forward and Becky's starting center," his older brother Mickey snapped.

Maggie Maitland put a restraining arm on each of them. "Knock it off, or you both will be doing hard time in your room tonight," she told them firmly. "Look, there's Freddy."

Robin's face lit up. "Hey Freddy, over here." He jumped to his feet. "Freddy!"

Freddy waved back and hurried to join them.

"Why isn't Theo playing?" Robin asked him.

"Here we go again," Mickey groaned. "Mom, he's too little to come to games, you should keep him home." Mickey said to Freddy, "I told him Theo would be playing later."

"Coach is not going to show them both Maitlands until later," Mickey told his younger brother. "That is how basketball is played."

"When did you become an expert?" Robin answered. Being six years old and the youngest member of a fast-talking family, he knew he must hang tough, especially with Mickey.

The whistle blew. The ball was in play. Becky easily knocked the ball away from her opponent and passed to Janice, who was standing in the clear. Becky ran downcourt to receive the pass. She paused at the top of the key. Set, shoot! Score! The boys screamed *Becky* and their mother grinned.

When the first half ended Maplewood was leading 37–19.

"Can we go talk to Becky and Theo, Mom, please?"

"If they have time, they'll come over here," Mrs.

Maitland said to her younger son, as she did at every game—basketball, soccer, baseball. She didn't enjoy the games the way her husband and children did. But she believed in supporting her children in whatever they tried.

"What's Theo drinking?" Mickey asked, tugging at his mother's arm.

"What, dear?" Mrs. Maitland asked, her mind on cigarettes. There was no place in the gym to smoke.

"Orange juice," Freddy explained. "Theo's got this new theory that orange juice gives her leg muscles more jumping power."

"They drink orange juice at the Olympics." Mickey sighed with satisfaction.

"Hi, Mom, hey, Mickey, did you see my oopshoop dunk right before the buzzer sounded?" Theo rolled up on the balls of her feet. Her short dark hair was damp on her neck. Her face was flushed and her eyes glowed. "What a game! Hi, Freddy. We've got it in our back pocket!"

"Whose back pocket?" Becky bent to wrap an Ace bandage around her right knee. "It's like tossing a tennis ball into a peach basket, they shouldn't even have a team," she said, wiping the perspiration from her upper lip.

"Look at that bandage," Mickey said. "Just like Earl-the-Pearl!"

"Becky's been drafted by the pros." Theo chuckled. "Will you rub my shoulder, Freddy?" She sat on the bench below him and dropped her head onto her chest.

"You're all sweaty," Freddy complained. "Not like the girl in the Ivory commercial."

"When you look more like the Marlboro man we'll discuss it." Theo stretched and frowned at Becky's leg. "How come you're wearing an Ace, Beck? I don't need one."

Mrs. Maitland looked from Theo to Becky. From the time they were quite small, if one twin experienced something the other didn't—from a stomachache to a bad dream—each was surprised that she could feel different from the other.

"My leg felt a little tight, so Mrs. Hawkins thought it would help."

"Maybe you shouldn't be playing," Mrs. Maitland remarked absently, wondering what a tight leg meant.

"It's nothing, Ma. If everybody quit when they got a little cramp, the world would be filled with people sitting on their butts."

"Becky knows what she's doing." Mickey gazed at his sister proudly.

"Let's go, girls," the coach called.

"How many baskets you want, Robin?" Theo asked.

"Seven, all alone, no assists." He giggled.

"Make eight, Becky," Mickey called.

Two minutes left to play. Becky called time out and

rewrapped her bandage tighter. Her leg had the oddest sensation, as though it were pumped full of liquid and were going to burst.

"You're not concentrating," Theo hissed. She turned to shoot. As Theo's arm went up, the guard shook the ball away from her. The whistle blew. Theo, angry at such an obvious foul, whirled around.

Becky was lying on the floor, curled over her right leg.

The Englishtown girls backed away slowly; Theo ran to her sister. Maggie Maitland sprang toward her daughters. Becky was shaking her head as though she had water in her ear. "It's so silly, it just gave out."

"Don't try to stand." Mrs. Hawkins looked at Mrs. Maitland. "I think we should call an ambulance—"

"No, it's nothing, c'mon." Becky looked agitated.

"Please call one, Mrs. Hawkins. Theo, call your father, tell him to meet us at the hospital, get the boys, I'll go in the ambulance."

"I'm going with Becky," Theo insisted, absently rubbing her right thigh.

"You stay with the boys at home," her mother told her.

"Mom, I'm OK," Becky said. Later she would remember that everyone thought it was the knee cartilage causing the swelling.

Coach Hawkins blew her whistle. "Since we have less than two minutes left on the clock, the game will be considered official, Maplewood winning 62–

38. You all played well."

No one applauded as the girls filed silently off the court.

"Which of them is it?" Theo heard while she waited for her father to come to the phone.

"Hope it wasn't Becky. She's the whole team."

"No, that's Theo, she's much faster."

Theo could think only of Becky's leg. She wished she could unzip Becky's skin, peer inside to see what was wrong.

"Dad? Theo. Becky fell on her leg—"

"Is she all right? Is she in pain?"

At the sound of his voice Theo began to cry. "You know Becky, she wants to finish the game."

"OK, darling, now stop crying."

"Sorry, Dad. Mom says to meet them at the hospital."

"I'll be there as soon as I can. Now don't lose control, everything's going to be fine."

By the time Theo got back to the gym two paramedics were lifting Becky onto a stretcher. She looked mortified.

"Hey, Becky, you look like a float in the Rose Bowl Parade," Theo shouted. Becky smiled.

"It feels numb—I never felt anything, I was running, then the leg simply wasn't there," Becky repeated.

"I want to go too." Robin pushed past the other people.

"None of that," Mrs. Maitland said firmly. "You

mind Theo, we'll call as soon as we know anything."

Theo's heart squeezed like a fist as she watched them wheel Becky away from her.

Mrs. Maitland crouched in the back of the ambulance, worked her fingers through the elastic bandage, pleating and stretching it.

"Mom, I am OK, you look gray, calm down."

"Last time Mickey broke his arm skiing. I won't survive four childhoods. Why don't you all sit quietly till you grow up?" Maggie smiled weakly.

"You'd hate us hanging around all the time," Becky told her. "Think of a lifetime of rainy days with us complaining 'There's nothing to do, Mom'!"

An X-ray technician greeted them at the emergency room. "Who do we have here? Not Becky Maitland!"

Becky wished she could jump off the stretcher. She felt so helpless.

"Dr. Seward called. He wants us to take the pictures. He'll be along as soon as he can." The attendant settled Becky on the table and positioned the machine. Becky knew her mother was chain-smoking in the waiting room.

Her parents would insist Becky stay home all weekend. Jay would be furious. He had been restless for the past few weeks, resenting any time spent with Theo or their other friends. She knew he had envisioned Mt. Columbine as nature's motel.

As the technician changed the angle of the machine Becky chewed her nails. How could she have been so clumsy? She and Jay had been looking forward to the weekend for so long. Perhaps if they had to postpone it Freddy and Theo would lose interest in the trip. Maybe the accident was a blessing in disguise.

Theo set the table, made a salad and peeled potatoes. She had a premonition that something was terribly wrong. Becky hadn't been tripped; she hadn't fallen after a jump under the basket. The leg had stopped working. She glanced at the clock; an hour and a half, still no word. She would wait another fifteen minutes. Then she'd call the hospital. She lowered the temperature of the oven so the chicken wouldn't dry out. Sighing heavily she sat down in her mother's chair at the table.

"I want her to stay off the leg," Dr. Seward told the Maitlands. "Keep it elevated this evening, ice bags on both sides of the leg. Her X rays are clear. You gave us a scare, Becky. When I spoke with Mrs. Hawkins on the phone, I thought you might have broken it."

"I told them it was nothing; there would be pain if it was broken," she said.

"I'll stop by to see you tomorrow, Becky."

"It'll be fine then, Dr. Seward."

"Does it hurt?" Mickey approached the couch with

his hands clasped behind him. "Need more ice?"

"Take the ice packs inside to Mom, I'm close to frostbite."

"No, let me," Robin said. "I want to do something."

"Time for bed, boys," their father announced.

They disappeared without a fuss.

"Poor old Robin, all through dinner he stared at me as though he expected one of my ears to fly across the table." Becky shifted around on the couch.

Theo slammed her history book shut. "Stay put, Becky."

"I can't write on my lap. I need a table," she snapped.

Becky swung her left leg to the floor.

"Stay where you are. Or better still, why don't you go to bed?" Theo sighed. "I didn't mean to snarl. I'll help you."

"Maybe I will. All that ice made me tired."

Once she was settled in bed, Becky felt better. In bed no one expected her to stand or walk.

"You OK?" Theo asked.

"Stop asking me that, I'm swell."

"You mean swoll," her sister answered.

Becky grimaced. "Bad, Theo." Becky turned out the light. "Guess backpacking is out. Jay will be really pissed."

"Tough for Jay. You didn't fall on purpose. We can push everything up till next weekend."

"Oh, Theo!" Becky wailed. "I didn't call Jay. He doesn't even know I fell."

"Are you kidding? It's probably all over school by now."

"He would have called."

"All day tomorrow kids will be flapping about— 'How's Becky?' 'Tell Becky hi,' 'Where's Becky?' " Theo answered calmly. "And Jay will be over here like a shot as soon as last period's over. You'll be a heroine. Take advantage of it. You won't get another chance like this!"

At least Jay and I won't have to sleep in separate sleeping bags to keep up appearances on Columbine, Becky consoled herself. The more she thought about it, the more she realized she had been dreading that charade.

Two

"Is it OK, your leg?" Mickey shook his sister's shoulder.

"Give me a break, Mickey," Becky growled. "It isn't even light yet."

"Is there someone in this room who isn't supposed to be?" Theo asked from under the covers. "He's going to wish he wasn't."

Mickey backed away from Becky's bed. "Are you OK?"

Invariably Becky melted at the sight of her brothers in their sagging pajamas printed with cowboys and bucking broncos. Mickey blinked at the bed light Theo snapped on. "It's almost six," he said defensively. "I woke up afraid something was wrong, then I remembered your leg."

Becky kicked off her blanket. "See, it's fine." She

sat on the edge of her bed. "Let's see if I can stand on it." She lined up her feet carefully as though they were shoes. She stood slowly. Her leg throbbed.

"It still hurts, doesn't it?" Theo asked.

"A little, but go back to bed, Mick. I'm fine."

"Can I sleep in here with you?"

Becky moved over and swung her legs back into the bed. "Come here, give me a hug." She squeezed him.

"Glad you're OK," Theo grumbled. "I hope Mom doesn't tell Grandma. She'll make a fuss."

"Which grandma?" Mickey asked.

"Both," Becky told him. "Nothing turns them on like sickness!"

By tightening the muscles in her calf Becky could walk without much pain. She tried to downplay the situation because Grandma Bacon was calling every night from Florida, asking about *developments* with the leg. Grandma Maitland had another line. "Are you telling me everything? Don't spare my feelings, darling, if it's a broken leg, I'll find out sooner or later."

Becky took it as a sign from Heaven when Coach Hawkins was called out of town. Becky didn't feel up to playing. Yet she felt better when nobody asked her about the pain. She realized that the unpredictability of the pain frightened her. If she had a cold or sore throat she knew from past colds what the aches would be like, when she'd feel better. But this elusive pain slithered along one side of her leg, then along the other. If she woke thinking about it, it would have disappeared during the night. If she forgot and ran across the street, it resurfaced with almost impish insistence.

A comment of Jay's haunted her. "Come on, Becky, I signed on for a complete lady, in full working order."

"It all works, buster."

"I hope we can get to Columbine next week, darlin'. Trying to be alone with a twin is like catching a goldfish with a lasso."

"You're telling me. People think being twins means having a copy of yourself, a double, someone exactly like you."

"You are identical, except for your body, which is a lot sexier than Theo's."

"And don't you forget it."

"Do you tell her what it's like, I mean, do you two talk about what you and I do?"

"Of course not," she said vehemently. "We don't tell each other everything anymore. We did when we were little, but things change, even for twins."

Becky had almost told Theo several times how much she adored Jay. But she didn't know how to win Theo over. If she said what she felt—"Jay is magic—as though my head's been stuffed with stars, as though my skin glittered, set to twinkling"—poetic gibberish like that would turn Theo sarcastic. Becky could hear her say "All that glitters is not gold," and dismiss Jay with a shrug. Becky preferred to avoid the subject and act good-natured when Theo gibed at her about Jay, rather than to confess that she hated Theo's putting him down. Especially since Freddy Simmons was no way a star in anyone's book.

Four more days and the leg still hadn't healed. Four more mornings Becky had pushed her tired body out of bed. On the fifth day Becky tried a tentative lay-up in the bathroom, behind the closed door. She had lost the spring in her legs. She turned away from her chalky reflection in the mirror. The truth was she couldn't have beaten a sixth grader in a one-on-one.

Theo usually spotted a missing eyelash on her twin. But she hadn't picked up on Becky's slowed pace. Becky pinched some color into her cheeks and wondered how long she could hide her clumsiness from Theo.

"I suppose we have to practice all weekend even though Coach won't be back till next weekend." Theo's voice was muffled. She was fighting her way out of a T-shirt. Its sleeves were twisted and tangled. She tossed it onto the heap of clothes on her bed.

"As a matter of fact I don't want to practice at all. I'm going to hang out with Jay."

"Well, smear me with jam and tie me to an ant-hill."

Becky enjoyed Theo's surprise. "I keep telling you on a scale of one to ten, my Jay is a definite fourteen!"

[23]

Becky blushed. She was delighted to be free of the game. Until Coach returned she would have long delicious hours with Jay. "The last thing Jay wants to play with me is basketball."

"Just be sure he closes his mouth if it rains—" Theo broke off. "I'm sorry. I'm so used to zinging at Jay I don't mean it. It's habit." Theo swept the pile of clothes onto the floor. "He could be a monkey, and if he made you happy, I'd peel bananas for him."

"I'll tell you about *happy*. I'd give up basketball, I'd give up a gold medal at the Olympics to be with Jay." As she spoke Becky's slender hands smoothed the wrinkles in the sheet. A few more quick movements and her bed was made.

Theo collapsed on her own tangled bed. "Even when she's oozing about love she makes the bed," Theo addressed the ceiling. "But speaking of gold medals"—she reached for a bag underneath her bed—"you should know by now I read your every thought."

"What the hell does that mean?" Becky asked, wary of the serious tone in Theo's voice.

"Words fly out of my mouth like insects—sometimes you get butterflies and sometimes mosquitoes." Theo pulled a shirt from its tissue-paper wrapping. "Ta-da!"

Becky admired the purple T-shirt with a gold Olympic medallion on the front. Theo unwrapped an identical one.

Becky sat down on the bed. "I thought we agreed not to dress twinnish anymore."

"I know. But you see, when I saw the shirt I thought it would be perfect for you, but I wanted one too."

Becky nodded. "The old one-two." She pulled on the new shirt and hugged Theo. Seeing how happy their identical reflections made her twin, Becky realized she had been right in keeping the details of her relationship with Jay from Theo. They were not running at the same pace anymore. She wondered how long it would take Theo to understand that.

For almost three weeks Becky had been slacking off more and more. Theo blamed Jay for Becky's lackluster performance. Jay was jealous of Becky's stardom and was subtly niggling at her to scale down her triumphs, so he would appear shinier. What a lowlife, Theo thought as Becky sat out most of the game against Durmatt. Becky had excuses almost every day for missing practice. She hadn't even worked out while the coach was away.

"Aren't you going to play at all?" Theo muttered to Becky.

Her twin smiled blandly. "Monthlies."

"Since when did you develop cramps?" Theo snapped.

"Since now." Becky had seized upon that ace among woman's complaints as a final excuse to keep from putting her leg to the test. She was so tired by lunchtime every day she couldn't have played basketball even if her leg had felt normal.

When Theo came upstairs after dinner Becky was sitting at her dressing table. Theo leaned across her twin and stuck her tongue out at their reflections. "Can't wait till the boys are old enough to do the dishes."

"And the vacuuming and the laundry." Becky chuckled. "Wonder what the big deal is tonight. Jay said he had a surprise, so we won't be going to the show with you and Freddy."

"Maybe his parents bought him a car." Theo rummaged through her sweater drawer.

"Not a chance. They don't have that kind of money. Besides they don't trust him. When we're watching TV in the basement his mother comes downstairs to check on us."

"Score one for Mrs. Cook." Theo disappeared inside the bathroom.

Becky rose from the dressing table and gasped. She sat down on her bed to massage her leg. It burned, as though hot liquid had been poured inside it. The skin was cool; there was no swelling. She must be imagining the pain. Ignore it, think about Jay and his surprise. Tightening the calf muscles Becky walked downstairs, concentrating on Jay, saying his name over and over in her mind.

Jay, always uncomfortable around Becky's father, looked as though someone had planted him next to the fireplace and forgotten to water him.

"Come on, sorry to keep you waiting."

They hurried out to the car.

"You limping again?" Jay asked, his eyes darting.

"Let's forget my leg, OK?"

"Great with me." He closed the door and went around to the driver's side. To Becky he looked like a TV anchorman.

"What's the mystery?" Becky asked, almost apologetically.

"You'll find out."

A few blocks from his parents' house, Jay pulled into a dead-end street. He turned off the engine and put his arm around Becky.

"We got our football rings yesterday. I want my lady to have it. Give me your hand, love."

"It's so heavy," Becky said. "And so big."

"Wear it on your thumb."

"I'll look like a fool."

"Just till we can go to the jeweler. He can make it smaller."

"But then it won't fit you," she said.

"I don't want to wear it, it's for you."

"What if you want it back?"

"Come on, Becky, don't be a down."

"I love it, and I love you, and I love the football team for letting you play varsity and it's the best thing that's ever happened to me." Becky felt more energetic than she had in weeks. Maybe all she needed was this proof of Jay's caring for her.

"My parents are in New York at the theater. I

am on my honor not to bring you to the house."

"What are we waiting for?" Becky leaned back against the seat and sighed happily.

Theo was rubbing her hair dry with a large towel when Becky burst into their room.

"What a night!" Becky held up her left hand and pointed to her thumb. "It was too big even for my middle finger."

Theo examined the ring and wondered at Becky's glee. "How come? I mean what made you take it? Rings are so *predictable*!" She broke off. "I'm really happy for you, Becky."

"Do you mind?" Becky asked hesitantly.

"Because I don't have Freddy's? Freddy says rings are bush."

"I'd be more impressed if Freddy *had* a ring," Becky snapped.

"Cool off. I won't put down the ring to anyone—Becky's got Jay Cook's football ring, just like *American Graffiti*, high-school romance, tra-la." Theo tossed her towel into the air. "How am I doing so far?"

Becky blushed. "I know it's Harriet High School—"

Theo snorted. "It's super. I'd wear one if someone gave me one." Theo hugged her sister. "Wait till Dad sees it! He'll want to know what it *means*."

"What does this ring mean?" Dick Maitland asked the following morning at breakfast. "Are you engaged? Must I prepare a dowry of three oxen and a herd of sheep?"

"Legally you need only provide the sheep and a couple of chickens," Becky answered solemnly.

"What does a ring mean these days?" asked their mother, patting her bathrobe pockets in search of a pack of cigarettes.

"I suppose, that we are special to each other."

"Vague, awfully vague," her father complained. "But so long as this boy doesn't get carried away, think this gives him exclusive rights to Becky—"

"I'll clear the table, in honor of the occasion." Theo jumped up, eager to elude her own thoughts. Perhaps she was a bit jealous; she had been dating Freddy longer and there was not even the glint of a ring in their relationship.

The doorbell rang, sending Mickey and Robin running. "Maybe it's Jay, I bet he wants to check up on the ring," Mickey yelled.

"Maybe he wants it back." Robin's face reappeared in the dining room. "It's Jay."

"We're having breakfast," Dick Maitland said sourly.

"Yes, come in, Jay." Maggie Maitland lit a cigarette and shook her head warningly to her husband. "Don't mind Mr. Maitland, he's not human on Sunday mornings," she added, as though that were an asset.

Theo brought the coffeepot to the table. "Have another cup of kindness, Dad." She glanced at Jay. He was tall, almost filled the doorway. His hair was so dark it looked silvery in the morning sunshine. She didn't think he had a lasting face. He looked like an actor in a soap opera—interchangeable channel to channel. What chilled Theo was that Jay's clichéd beauty turned Becky into a soap-opera girl when she was with him.

"Sorry if I sounded gruff. I see congratulations are in order, or shouldn't I say that?" Mr. Maitland reached for the plate of sticky buns and held it out to the boy. "Have a piece of cake. Becky, get him a plate."

Jay stared at the proffered plate. "I ate. Thanks."

The Maitlands looked at him expectantly.

"Oh, I came for Becky. Skating rink's open. Theo too, of course."

Theo wondered if Becky's wearing the ring meant Jay would include Theo like punctuation at the end of every thought.

"I'll pass," she said, noting that Becky was blushing.

Maggie Maitland smiled. "Perhaps you'll stay for dinner, Jay?"

"Dinner?" he asked as though he had never heard of the meal. He backed out of the room. Becky muttered good-byes and followed him.

"Are we going to squirm in our own house because Becky is toting that boy's ring?"

"Nobody's squirming, Dick. They're just a bit uncomfortable. It's new to them."

"I doubt it. He's probably got a handful of rings,

probably got a girl in every high school in the county."

"That's giving Becky a lot of credit," Theo said and took some dirty plates to the kitchen.

"This is better than TV," Robin said happily.

It is TV, Theo thought.

"You boys go brush your teeth and tidy your room."

"You always say that." Mickey sighed heavily.

" 'Comes with being a mother,' " Robin mimicked.

When Becky came home from the rink, Theo noticed she was limping slightly. "Your leg hurting again?"

"Not used to skating. You should have come. Rusty was making a fool of herself, pretending to be Dorothy Hamill."

"What did they say about your ring?"

"Nothing. Rusty said I was lucky, as though I had won him in the lottery."

"Bet Carmela will cry crocodile tears of joy, that golden Becky got Carmela's favorite boy."

"It hurts almost all the time now."

"What does?" Theo asked absently.

Becky sat next to Theo on the bed. "My leg. First it was numb, then it throbbed. I figured it was the fall, but it's been three weeks, and now it *burns*."

"Burns?"

Becky leaned her head on her sister's shoulder and began to cry. "What could it be?" She couldn't stop crying.

"Mom," Theo screamed. "Mom, come quick."

"No, no, I don't want them to know." Becky wept. "I can't fix it."

Mrs. Maitland ran up the stairs. "What's wrong, Theo?"

"What's everybody yelling about?" Mr. Maitland appeared a few seconds after his wife. "Becky! It's that boy. What has he done?" Her father rushed to her.

"Daddy, it's not Jay. It's her leg, it *burns*." Theo began to cry too. "It's been hurting her all this time."

"Is it your leg?" Maggie knelt in front of Becky.

"Why didn't you say something," her father said, pacing the room. "We should have taken you back to Dr. Seward."

"He said the X rays were clear, they took X rays," his wife said.

"I'll call him and say it's an emergency." Dick Maitland rushed from the room.

Mrs. Maitland lit one cigarette after another on the way to the doctor's office. Becky twisted the ring on her thumb and bit her lip. "It doesn't feel sprained," she repeated several times. "I don't know what it could be," she appealed to Theo.

"What do we know about Sawbones Seward anyway? Dad, maybe he's a quack."

"Theo," her father said threateningly.

"Just trying to lighten things up."

Dr. Seward examined Becky's leg and took blood

and urine samples. "I'll call you as soon as we get these back from the lab," he said gravely. "You should have told us sooner, Becky."

"What could it be?"

"I want to have it X-rayed," he spoke over the girls' heads to their parents.

"But they X-rayed it a few weeks ago," Mrs. Maitland said irritably. Couldn't he keep his patients straight? Maybe they should take Becky to a different doctor. She tried to get her husband's attention.

"Maybe she should see someone in New York." He had read her mind.

"Yes, that might be a good idea," Maggie added quickly. "Not that we don't have full confidence in you, Dr. Seward."

Three days later they were in the Park Avenue office of an orthopedic surgeon. Becky's eyes were wide with fright. Mrs. Maitland held her daughter's hand but said nothing. Mr. Maitland pushed his lips in and out and arranged the magazines in the waiting room in alphabetical order. "Comes from being a librarian." He smiled apologetically to the receptionist.

The doctor examined Becky, studied the X rays they had brought with them and asked them to wait outside. Five minutes later the receptionist asked Becky's parents to come into the office, but suggested Becky might like to wait in the reception area. "It's *my* leg," she said, her voice quavering.

[33]

"Becky can hear whatever you have to say," Mrs. Maitland told Dr. Titelbaum. It did not occur to her that he might say anything too terrible for her daughter to hear.

"Very well." He waited till they were all seated. Becky gripped the cool metal of the chair frame. "Becky has a growth about the size of a small orange." He smiled. "We'll do a biopsy to see if the cells are malignant."

"Dear God." Maggie Maitland gritted her teeth. I must not cry in front of Becky.

"How could this happen?" Dick Maitland asked. "Are you sure?"

The doctor shrugged. "There are many variables in a tumor of this kind; it may be a sarcoma, but it might be a benign mass that's been sitting there for years. Hard to tell in someone Becky's age." Dr. Titelbaum selected a pencil from the mug on his desk and tapped it against his opposite palm.

"It hasn't felt numb this week, maybe it's going away by itself," Becky said, pulling her legs back under her chair.

"Biopsy's a simple procedure. You'll be in the hospital two days. We want to move as quickly as possible in a case of this nature. My nurse is arranging with Mercy Hospital for you to be admitted this afternoon."

"No!" Becky cried. "I can't today."

The doctor nodded. "Don't worry. It's a simple procedure. We have to find out what we're dealing with before we can make you well."

Why does he sound so reasonable, she thought angrily. "What will you do if it is a tumor?" she asked in a whisper.

"Let's cross that bridge later on," he said.

I bet he's said that a thousand times, Maggie thought as she embraced her trembling daughter.

"Everything's going to be fine," Dick Maitland said fiercely. He covered his face with his hands. He saw a large bird hovering overhead, the bird's powerful wings cast shadows over Becky and Maggie. The bird was dashing at his face, those fierce wings beating against his shoulders. Through a crack between his trembling fingers, he caught the bird's ugly stare. The bird meant to peck out his heart. He rushed forward to protect his wife and child from the devil's disease-bearing crow.

Three

The first morning of kindergarten a well-meaning teacher had separated Becky and Theo. The teacher had sold the Maitlands on the importance of developing each twin's individuality. I want Becky, Theo had shouted. Becky had refused to speak at home or at school until Becky and Theo were allowed to be together again.

I want Becky, Theo shouted silently. I must not panic, she'll be home day after tomorrow.

Theo hugged her brothers and fixed them peanut-butter snacks as though Becky were at a late practice or out jogging. "Freddy's got the car, so we can eat at Happyburger and go to the movies at the shopping center. How about that for a piece of good news?" Theo said, clapping her hands like a cheerleader.

"It's a school night," Mickey reminded her.

"But I'm in charge," Theo grinned. "Becky and Mom and Dad are probably eating in some hotshot French restaurant so we should have fun too." Her heart pounded. Silently she begged Becky to forgive her this lie. Mom had said the hospital was quite cheery and Becky had a TV and some magazines. Sitting home wouldn't help Becky get through the night, Theo decided. She had never had to make decisions without Becky.

"Hey, guys, we have Becky to thank for tonight." Freddy opened the car door.

Theo gave him a filthy look. "It's not exactly her choice, Freddy. She has to have some tests early in the morning."

"Sorry, Theo, you know what I meant. I think the chicken place is having a Wednesday-night special. Think you boys could eat apple pie *and* ice cream?"

"Yeah!" they shouted. Freddy started the car and they drove off singing Beatles songs.

Becky was relieved when her parents finally left. Pretending to be calm and serene was a strain. Of course it's nothing, it's just a precaution, better to be thorough, it's the best hospital in the world, look at all that equipment, even get your own TV, not that you'll be here long enough to enjoy it. So much false heartiness! She and her father grinned at each other with the virtuous enthusiasm of a family advertising bran cereal.

The curtain had been drawn between Becky and

the girl who occupied the other half of the room. As soon as her parents had left, Becky got out of bed and swung the curtain back. "Do you mind? Am I disturbing you?" Becky wondered about the bottles hanging from a metal rack over the girl's bed. A colorless fluid was dripping through plastic tubing into the girl's arm. Becky sensed that one didn't ask questions in a hospital. Only an hour in these foreign surroundings but she had grasped that blatant questions were taboo. Nurses smiled evasively; social workers bounced around like cheerleaders.

"No, nothing good on TV, everything's repeats." The girl was flipping the pages of a magazine with her free hand. "I'm Sally Beth Babbit."

"Hi, Becky Maitland. I'm having a biopsy in the morning."

"I'm in for chemo."

"Chemo?" Becky kept her voice low. She didn't want Sally Beth to see how frightened she was. She wished she had Theo's ease talking to strangers.

"Medicine," she held up her arm, which was strapped to a board. Plastic tubing coiled close to her wrist. "We live too far away for me to get it as an outpatient."

Becky nodded, mystified. Sally Beth's skin was chalky, her lips almost blue. She was wearing a scarf wrapped tightly around her head, hiding her hair. Becky wondered how to circumvent the forbidden "Why are you here?"

[38]

"Who's your doctor?" Sally Beth asked a few minutes later.

"What *is* his name, I only met him today, he's not our regular doctor, you see I fell on the basketball court a few weeks ago—"

"McNally, Maxwell, Garvey, Titelbaum, Tang, O'Donnell?" Sally reeled off the names quickly.

"That's it, Titelbaum, the surgeon."

"I know him. The leg man. McNally's the chest surgeon. I know most of them by sight."

"You must have been here a long time."

"Only five days this time, but two years if you count all my clinic time."

Becky couldn't imagine an illness that lasted two years.

"Want to go down to the Playroom? They have crafts projects."

"Are we allowed?" Becky looked at Sally Beth's bottles.

"Sure. They didn't tell you to stay in bed did they?"

The girl's abrasiveness comforted Becky after the blank smiles and reassurance of the staff. "I assumed in a hospital you stay in bed."

Sally Beth sat up and swung her legs over the side of the bed. "Over there in the corner, can you get my wheelchair?"

"I've never wheeled anybody, what if, well, those bottles, aren't you scared they'll break?"

"I've done this hundreds of times." Sally Beth settled herself into the wheelchair. Becky thought of the rocking seats of a Ferris wheel and wished there were a safety bar to protect Sally Beth. Very slowly she turned the wheelchair, her eyes never leaving the bottles. They swung just enough for the liquid to slosh gently against the glass.

Once they were out in the hall Becky felt better. The walls were the same dark-green–light-blue combination as the corridors at school. Even the dark-patterned linoleum floor looked familiar.

"Turn left here, it's that double door at the end of the hall."

"Aren't there any other patients but you and me?"

"The little kids are probably in bed and everybody else is either in the Playroom or in private rooms."

"What disease rates a private room?"

"It's for very sick kids."

Becky could contain herself no longer. "What do they have?"

Sally Beth turned around and studied Becky's face. Satisfied that Becky was sincerely confused, Sally Beth waved her free hand. "Ask your doctor tomorrow."

Becky opened the door and was surprised by the bright lights and Bee Gee records playing loudly at the other end of the huge square room. A boy in a wheelchair was shooting pool. As she wheeled Sally Beth closer she saw the boy had only one leg. Several girls were sitting in wheelchairs wearing scarves tied like Sally Beth's.

A heavyset girl in a pink nylon pants suit came

toward them. She looked like a gym teacher. "Hello, I'm Dottie. We have kits to make ashtrays and plaques, you can paint tiles or do baskets."

"She's only in for a biopsy, Dottie," Sally Beth explained.

Becky went over to the crafts table where a girl about seven years old was sitting in a wheelchair that was three sizes too large for her spindly body. Becky stared at her, unable to determine what made her appear so strange.

The girl was intent on the piece of wood she was staining. She caught Becky staring at her. Becky gasped. The child was bald.

Turning around she saw the one-legged boy hunched over his pool cue. Sally Beth's hand reached for hers. "Want to meet any of the kids?"

Becky looked down at her. Her skin was the color of skim milk. That bluish tinge frightened Becky. She ran from the Playroom. Once in the hall she didn't know how to get back to her room. She glanced into the doorway of the first room she passed. A nurse was adjusting more of those mysterious bottles. The aluminum poles were beginning to look like trees to Becky, horrid trees bearing those bottles as their threatening fruit.

"Nurse, nurse!" she called.

The woman came toward her. "What's the matter, are you ill?" the nurse asked.

"Of course not. I'm here for a biopsy," Becky said nervously. "I mean I'm not sick, like these kids. I can't find my room, only a biopsy, I fell on the basket-ball court, I'm going home day after tomorrow."

The woman checked the bracelet tag on Becky's wrist.

"Room A27. That's the other corridor, you're on the wrong side of the ward." The nurse smiled and spoke into an intercom. "Aide to B19, aide to B19." A black girl in a yellow-striped dress came hurrying along the corridor. She looked like a giant bumble-bee.

"Would you take Becky back to A27? She's a bit turned around. Good luck tomorrow, Becky." She turned back to the room.

"The kid in there, what's wrong with him?" Becky asked the aide.

She shrugged. "They don't tell me, besides I work on A, your side. You'll get used to it in a few days."

Becky shook her head. "Not me. I'm only here for a biopsy."

The girl made a noncommittal grunt and settled Becky into her bed. "Didn't they tell you how to ring the buzzer and where the Playroom is? Some-times we get so busy—would you like some juice? The cart will be around later, but I could get you some now."

"No thanks. What time do they do biopsies any-way?"

"You'll have to ask your doctor. Don't worry, they won't start without you." The girl grinned. Hospital humor, Becky thought wryly, is about on a par with Robin's jokes.

"Say, is this my phone, can I call my sister?"

"Just dial 9—didn't they tell you nothing?" The girl shook her head. "Day staff leaves everything for us. This buzzer clipped to the sheet, you push it if you need help. After a while they be in to give you a pill, so you'll sleep; if you need assistance you buzz." She spoke rapidly, mechanically, eyeing the can of nuts on Becky's table.

"We live in Jersey, can I call there?"

"OK, long distance you dial 0, might as well take your temp, long as I'm standing here." She reached for the chart at the foot of the bed. "You have anything to drink since supper?"

Becky shook her head. She could barely wait to talk to Theo. "Nurse will be in with your medication." The girl asked her a couple more times if she wanted juice and left.

Becky settled back to talk to Theo. How she wished her sister were sitting on the end of the bed. The phone rang for several minutes but there was no answer. Theo and the boys must have beat it to the movies. She wondered if she would have skipped off for a good time if Theo was in the hospital. She thought not.

Becky thought about calling Jay. He thought her parents were making a big production about rushing her into New York to see this doctor. When she told him she was in a hospital, he would probably make fun of all the Maitlands. Jay was unable to offer comfort. Whenever she was down, he would glower at her or fall silent, forcing her to abandon her own feelings and attend to him.

Balancing the pros and cons of telling Jay, Becky thought how extraordinary her situation was. It was no routine dentist appointment. He'd be furious if she didn't tell him.

"Hi, Jay, guess where I am!"

"Your mother's room?"

"A hospital room!"

"Come off it."

"It's true. The doctor found something *suspicious.* Tomorrow they're doing a biopsy."

"New York doctors put you in the hospital just for the bread. They got to keep their swimming pools filled."

"Not this guy." Becky giggled. "He's got such a mean face he'd sink like a stone. And the other girl in the room with me is gross. She's got tubes and bottles—not from this planet!"

"When are you coming home?"

"Day after tomorrow."

"Didn't he say what's wrong with you?"

"That's why they're doing the biopsy. But he didn't seem uptight. My folks aren't worried."

"Of course not. You're the one going under the knife. My father says—"

"Cut it out, Jay," Becky squealed. "This guy's cutting me open tomorrow. It might be serious. Aren't you upset? Just a little? Maybe I have a wrecked knee from all the basketball."

"You're not exactly Bill Walton! You know what my old man thinks—doctors have the cure for cancer but are suppressing it to make a few bucks, a few *billion* bucks."

"Shut up about your *father*! I'm the one trapped in this awful hospital—Jay, I feel like they've stolen my body. I'm not *me* here."

"Listen to me, darlin'. You're going to be fine. Think about last weekend."

"And next weekend, when I get home." Becky giggled. "Invasion of much better body snatchers."

"I love you, Becky, you're my lady."

Becky hung up the phone and pulled the blanket up. She wished they'd do the biopsy now so she could go home to Jay. Even Sally Beth wheeling herself into the room couldn't lower Becky's spirits. *I love you, Becky,* he had said. She felt sorry for the girl and at the same time relief that she herself wasn't very sick. A painful leg would not separate her from Jay. *I love you, Becky, you're my lady. . . .*

"You look awfully smug. How come you left the Playroom? Did Kathy say something? She's got a tongue like a scalpel."

"She's bald," Becky said, not caring anymore for politeness. She'd never see Sally Beth or Kathy again.

Sally Beth snorted and snatched the scarf from her head. "So am I, it's the drugs. Hair comes out in gumps, you wake up in the morning and your bed's filled with hair, your pillow, it's all over my T-shirts and sweaters, like a dog shedding." She rubbed her head, which gleamed horribly under the fluorescent light.

"How do you stand it?"

"I don't have a choice. Kathy's got the bad kind, one of the nurses told me."

"The bad kind?" What stories she'd have for Jay!

Sally Beth nodded. "Myelocytic. It's the chronic adult form, a bummer when kids get it. Most kids get acute forms." She broke off. "I'll probably get roasted for running off at the mouth. The staff don't think we know shit from Shinola. But I go to the library at home and read up. Of course it's not as current as medical stuff, but fat chance me getting near medical books. Since my mother won't even say the word in front of me."

"I don't have a clue what you're talking about."

"Leukemia," the other girl said sharply.

Becky gasped. "Kathy has leukemia?"

"So do I," she said calmly. "And so do most of the kids on this floor."

"But you said you've been sick two years, you go to school—" Becky wanted to pull the curtain. She smiled, aware that the smile carried no conviction.

"It's not catching," Sally Beth said.

"I'm so sorry." Becky's voice quavered. Whyever had they put her in the room with a girl who was dying? No wonder she was so pale. Wait till Theo found out Becky had met someone with leukemia!

"This is a cancer ward," Sally Beth said.

"It's not just for cancer," Becky answered quickly.

Sally Beth snickered.

"Hi, girls. Got some blood for you, Sally Beth." The nurse hung a bag of blood from the pole and bent over the girl's arm. Becky turned her face to the wall. Cancer ward! What a bully! Acting like a medical researcher, knocking around all those strange words. She probably lied about leukemia. People with leukemia don't go to school. Wasn't it leukemia Ali MacGraw had in *Love Story?*

Four

"The procedure we follow at Mercy has been successful in an encouraging number of cases like your daughter's. We will proceed with an aggressive attack. Our current regimen is high-dose methotrexate with citrovorum rescue—"

"Citrovorum rescue?" Dick Maitland's voice was a squeak.

"Folinic acid to protect the normal cells as much as possible from the toxicity of the drug. We need a maximum toxicity, of course."

"Toxic? What about the rest of her body?" Becky's father asked, relieved that his own analytic tone of voice had returned.

"Good question. The normal cells are affected but at a slower rate. We administer citrovorum factor to counteract the toxicity to the normal cells. Of course some of the malignant cells are protected too—" Dr. Titelbaum leaned back in his chair and grinned disarmingly.

"Mrs. Maitland, your daughter has an excellent chance with my femur-replacement technique. The drugs destroy the malignant cells so completely that the femur becomes necrotic. That's when we replace it with a metallic prosthesis."

Maggie looked at the doctor sharply. "Isn't there a way, just with the drugs? Becky is a marvelous athlete, she's on all the varsity teams."

Bile stung Dick Maitland's throat. Necrotic? He envisioned a rotting bone withering into uselessness. How could this foul business be happening to them?

The surgeon's words were forming a choppy sea. Becky's father recoiled from the man's buoyant tone, so pleased about his surgical technique.

"If there are no metastases to other parts of the body—"

Maggie Maitland hunched her shoulders and bowed her head. "Becky's body, it's my daughter's body."

"—we will continue prophylactic chemo for a year or so."

"Two years," Mrs. Maitland gasped.

"Yep. We have to blast those malignant cells."

"Will she be normal, I mean have use of the leg? After all this business?" Maggie asked.

"We don't know, Mrs. Maitland. Each case is different."

He sounds like he's lecturing to a couple of half-wits. Why can't he break that facade and admit what a horror this business is? Maggie wondered.

But the doctor continued in well-modulated tones. "Each kid reacts differently." He replaced the pencils in the cup on his desk. "We must remember these years are frustrating for any adolescent. It's a time when people are growing into their bodies. To have your body turn on you is dismal indeed."

"She will recover?" Mr. Maitland asked, wishing he had not made it a question.

"We have patients with osteosarcomas who are alive five years after surgery."

"Five years?" Mr. and Mrs. Maitland looked at each other.

"This is a new procedure, we don't have enough data on patients' survival for longer than five years. If Becky's cancer has not spread, she has a better than good chance of recovery."

"But you're not sure? When will we know?"

"I'm afraid we don't know for certain." He reached for a stack of pages. "Here is a pamphlet on osteo tumors, some instructions for nutrition, and a list of common side effects of the drugs; we're going to start Becky off on methotrexate tomorrow. We'll keep her here for the first chemo, to monitor her carefully, see how she tolerates the drugs. The most visible side effects are weight loss and loss of hair," he said briskly. He stood up, making any further conversation impossible. "I'll look in on Becky later this afternoon. Would you like me to be with you when you tell her?"

"Yes, she may have some questions," Mr. Maitland said.

"No, we'll tell her alone." Mrs. Maitland wanted to give her daughter some privacy in which to scream and cry without the scrutiny of this stranger.

Becky was calm, Becky didn't cry. Perhaps it was because they didn't mention the surgery. They said she'd need drugs, which might make her throw up. She would probably lose some hair, she certainly didn't have cancer, of course she wasn't as sick as Sally Beth. Maybe they should have her moved to a different room so she wouldn't be around such a depressing girl.

Still numb from their own shock, it was the best Mr. and Mrs. Maitland could do. By the time the dinner trays were brought around, Becky had an aluminum pole bearing bottles of her own. She was still muzzy from the anesthetic, but she was alert enough to see her mother's eyes smudgy and dark. Her father was unnaturally animated, jumping to his feet like a host whenever a nurse or aide entered the room. Becky was too tired to wonder about her parents' behavior.

Mrs. Maitland would stay at the hospital with Becky and Mr. Maitland would go home. They would tell Theo everything they had told Becky. They would be vague with the boys. Above all they would insist the familiar routine of school and home activities not be altered. An attempt at normalcy would make Becky's condition seem less dangerous.

Sally Beth had been watching the Maitlands all day, lounging on top of her bed, pretending to watch TV. She had rejected all offers of diversions, including the Playroom and the movie being shown in the library.

"My mother works," she said as soon as Mr. Maitland had gone. "She used to stay when I first got sick, but we need the money, she works at a processing plant near Cherry Hill. When you've had it long as I have, chemo's no big deal anyway."

"When will you go home?" Maggie hoped her face didn't reflect her desire to get rid of Sally Beth, regardless of where her mother was.

"Tomorrow, unless my counts are very low. They've juiced me up on a lot of blood, so I should be OK."

Maggie detected a challenging note in the girl's voice. Spiteful little bitch trying to frighten me, she thought and straightened the covers around her sleeping daughter.

The nurse showed her the foldaway cot. Maggie had seen a number of other mothers walking the halls, but she had been too shy to talk to any of them in the Parents' Lounge, where she had retreated for desperately needed cigarettes. She wished Becky would wake up so she would have a reason for sitting in the room without talking to Sally

Beth. Becky looked paler than she had yesterday. She seemed so helpless, all curled up against the whiteness of the sheets and blanket. She'd buy Becky a colorful robe, she wished she had thought to buy a book or two that afternoon. She turned on the mini-TV suspended over Becky's bed. If Sally Beth hadn't been there she'd have stretched out on the bed with Becky, but it might be against hospital policy and she couldn't bear being reprimanded by Sally Beth.

"Why don't you sit on the bed, you can see better," Sally Beth said, not taking her eyes from her tiny screen.

"I don't want to disturb Becky."

"She'll be out all night if they hung methotrexate."

"Is it painful?" Mrs. Maitland asked.

"If vomiting your guts is painful."

Mrs. Maitland didn't answer. Sally Beth lowered the sound on her TV. "Some of us say the drugs are worse than the cancer."

"Please don't use that word," she said.

"Suit yourself. Old Humphrey, the senator who died? He called chemo bottled death."

Maggie fled to the nurses' station, the blood pounding in her ears. "You must put my child in another room. That girl is frightening her, I don't want to cause trouble, but try to understand, Becky is very sensitive."

The nurse nodded. "Believe me, Mrs. Maitland, we have a full house. We couldn't switch Becky to-

[53]

night for any reason, we've got three new admissions spending the night in the clinic facility downstairs because we don't have a spare bed. I'll talk to Sally Beth if you'd like."

"Never mind." She forced herself to walk toward the Parents' Lounge. Maybe some of the other mothers knew how to cope with surly roommates. If they were going to be coming to the clinic for tests or treatment every week Maggie must not rub the staff the wrong way. She mustn't handicap Becky with a pain-in-the-ass mother.

The Parents' Lounge was deserted. There was an acrid odor of stale cigarettes and plastic cups of oily coffee making the room even more dismal than its turquoise plastic chairs and bulletin board with outdated announcements for church services. A SMILE button was attached to the bulletin board and someone had tacked up a child's drawing of a healthy cell and a malignant cell. Maggie sat in the chair closest to the corridor. She lit a cigarette and listened to the muffled noises of the hospital settling down for the night. The fluorescent lights in the hall were dim; she couldn't imagine what the next few months would hold. She could recall no genuine tragedy in her life or her husband's. They knew no one with a chronic illness. There was a second cousin who had succumbed to a heart condition after he had had two mammoth coronaries. By the time he had died, everyone had been quite prepared. A chill swept over her. She hurried back to the room and kissed her sleeping child. She stroked Becky's arm lightly. The nurse had drawn the curtain protecting her from Sally Beth, but what if Becky should wake and see her mother crying?

I'd better start now. Discipline, strict exercise of will. Becky must not see my fear. I must convince her that she will get well. Maggie felt an urge to kidnap Becky, to shield her from the doctors and their drugs and machines and surgeons. What did any of these doctors know of Becky?

My daughter cries if she sees an animal dead in the road. We always say, "Don't look, Becky, there's an old rag on the highway." She loves to read aloud to her brothers while they work on their model planes. My daughter doesn't lie, she doesn't ridicule people, she doesn't deserve this.

Maggie wiped her eyes on a corner of the sheet and sat in the half-darkened room, the orange curtain making a silent tomb of the bed and its occupant. She reached for Becky's hand and examined the fingers gently curled against her own palm. Even her hands are pretty. My daughter doesn't have cancer, the doctor made an error.

On the phone Becky had talked about IV's and heparin locks. Theo couldn't find them in the dictionary. There were no medical books in the public library. Theo kept away from her friends even at school. Their laughter added to the pain she felt for Becky. The doctor said the drugs would not interfere with school. Drugs were going to destroy Becky's hair, and the doctor said chemo would not interfere with school.

Finally the car pulled into the driveway. Theo was out the door, running to Becky.

Becky did not leap from the car and run to meet her. Becky inched out of the backseat with her bad leg straight out in front of her. She lowered the leg to the ground, supporting it with her hands. Then she balanced on her crutches and walked to where Theo was standing.

"Please don't cry," Becky said flatly. She looked pale and her eyes were gray stones.

"I wasn't going to. But you may when you taste my meat loaf." Theo looked into Becky's eyes.

"I don't want any dinner," Becky said. She made her way slowly into the house.

Finally dinner was over. Becky had hardly touched her food. "Come on, Mom, I'll be big as a house, especially since I will be sitting on my gluteus maximus for the next few months."

"What's that?" Robin asked. He and Mickey had barely spoken since Becky had come home. Robin longed to try the crutches but he was afraid to ask.

"Your bee-hind, jerk," Mickey said.

"Talk like that and Dr. Titelbaum might come and give you chemo right in the house, Mick. You know you guys may have to get needles; and some of them are about a foot long. They make them up special for little brothers."

Theo pushed the food around on her plate. What did I expect, that we'd sit around in the dark weeping? That no one would eat or watch TV or take a bath? The boys are lucky, she thought as they whooped with glee at Becky's teasing. Her eyes filled with tears. She jumped up to clear the table.

Becky loved them all for trying so hard but the chatter made the tumor seem like an accepted member of the family. If she had the flu or even a garden-variety broken arm, everyone could afford to act glum. But one scrap of pity and the tumor would swell to encompass them all. She excused herself and limped to the bathroom. Under the sound of the toilet flushing she cried into a towel, its harsh texture comforting her like the lick of a cat's tongue.

Dick Maitland looked at his daughters' empty chairs and said to his wife over the boys' heads, "We need a demilitarized zone, I suspect."

Theo stacked the plates in the sink and wondered if Becky would want to talk about it. Becky wondered if it was fair to tell Theo how scared she was. After the boys went to bed Theo and Becky were reluctant to leave the neutrality of the living room.

"We made up Dad's den for you," Theo said. "I brought your dresser stuff down. What clothes do you want me to bring down?"

"I am not sleeping anywhere in this house but my own bed," Becky said, her face red with fury.

"Honey, it's not practical," her mother said.

"I am sleeping in my own bed."

"We will get you upstairs," Theo said and squeezed her twin's hand. She waited for Becky to position her leg and swing up onto the crutches.

"Stay here, Mom, Dad," Theo said decisively. "We'll do it ourselves."

"You take this crutch, and I'll use the banister," Becky told her.

"It will be easier if you leave the stiff leg out behind you like this." Theo crouched on the stairs with one leg behind her. "Then just crawl up—"

"No, look how your leg is bouncing. I can't."

"OK, I'll go behind you and hold the leg a few inches from the stairs."

"Don't let it drop, Theo."

"Wait a second. I'll take the crutches up and your books, then we'll be set."

"Be careful, don't drop the brace."

"Just keep moving, Becky. I know what I'm doing."

Inch by inch they advanced. At the top of the stairs, Becky turned around and sat on the top step until Theo maneuvered around her and got the crutches in position. "Operation mobility is a success, can't wait till the morning when we do the down side."

"Christ, Theo, I forgot about going down. I should have stayed in the den."

"Crapola. We'll do it exactly the same way. You'll crawl in reverse, backward down the stairs, you'll synchronize with me leading, as I guide the leg, you'll bring up the rear with the body." Theo grinned.

Becky slumped on her bed, lifting the leg up slowly, as though it were a separate being.

"This is lousy, Becky," Theo said from the depth of her closet. "Do you want to talk or should I shut up?"

"Have you said anything to Jay?"

"Of course not. He asked me what time you were coming home and I said you sounded drugged on the phone."

"I don't want to say it out loud." Becky twisted the ring on her thumb. The nurses had teased her about it, her lucky charm. They wouldn't let her wear it to the operating room.

"Maybe it would be easier if you practiced on Rusty or some of the other girls," Theo said gently.

"I don't want pity."

"It's only human for them to feel sorry for you. After all, it is awful."

"My roommate at the hospital has leukemia," Becky said flatly.

"That certainly is a powerful opening line." Theo laughed nervously.

"Mom gave her evil looks for using the word cancer." Becky continued to stare at Theo. "She told me she doesn't stay in touch with most of her friends. They are worrying about boys and she might not live till graduation."

Theo chewed her lip. "Leukemia's not what you have anyway."

"Help me take my pants off," Becky said, suddenly very tired.

Theo shuddered when she felt the metal brace under the soft beige flannel pant leg.

"Oh God! How can I tell Jay?"

"He won't care about the brace."

"Every night *I* had to call *him*. Yesterday I asked 'How come you can't ever call me?' You know what he said? 'I can't handle hospitals, Becky, I hate to think of my girl being examined by interns not much older than me.'"

"So play doctor with him." The color returned to Theo's face. "When he sees you sitting in the living room, just like always, he'll realize you are still Becky. The brace isn't you."

"Yes it is. That's the point." Becky lifted the braced leg onto the bed. "Mom and Dad hate to say it out loud as much as I do. Sally Beth set me straight. At first she terrified me, but I trust her now. She would never bullshit me. The staff glosses over the grisly details."

"I want to know the gritty part too. I want to go through it with you, Becky. The way we've shared everything else." Theo sat down next to Becky.

"After Titelbaum bombards the tumor with chemo, and the rest of me's *druggy*, then he cuts out the cancer."

"Don't let's talk about it now." Theo could not keep the dread from her voice.

"I've got bone cancer, Theo," Becky said flatly. "You don't. That's why we can't go through it together."

"Becky!"

"I can say it because *cancer* seems unreal. Something you read about, a disease other people get. Last week we didn't know I had it, so no one was afraid to say it. Cancer means old people dying—our version of the Black Plague."

Becky continued. "I feel like I'm in a room with no windows and a barricaded door. And the game is to see if I can find the way out."

"Don't say that!" Theo collapsed onto her bed.

"What the hell are you frightened of? I'm the one that's got to live through it."

"Maybe I've got it too."

Becky didn't answer. She had wished Theo had a tumor so she wouldn't have to describe the hospital, explain all the new terms. She had fantasies of Theo miraculously waking up with a companion cancer the size of a grapefruit. Then she prayed God would not punish her for such demonic thoughts. Please God, don't let me die, don't let Theo get sick, but God, please don't count me out of the game.

Her first morning back at school Becky had to see her guidance counselor. She had insisted her parents not come with her—she needed practice in handling people herself. Miss Quennell would be a good first try. She prided herself on believing whatever the students told her. As Becky had expected she was sympathetic and made none of the jokes Becky knew she'd get from the kids.

"I have a leg condition, *minor*, but the doctors just found it last week. I will need to miss school for treatments in New York," Becky said, surprised that the woman did not ask for any specifics. She asked several times how Becky felt, if she needed a glass of water. Then, as if sensing Becky's impatience, she became businesslike.

"With a record as good as yours, I know you won't want to fall behind your class. Not in your Senior year."

"No problem. I have a built-in tutor. Theo and I take the same classes. I would prefer, my family would prefer, if you would keep my illness confidential. I don't want everybody gossiping."

"We'll certainly try, Becky, but you know what the grapevine is like." Miss Quennell smiled. "You're coping well with whatever it is. Let's hope it will be cured soon."

Becky did not reply. She and Theo had perfected a story about a hairline fracture of her metatarsals ("The medical terms will snow them," Theo had chortled) to explain the crutches and the brace.

"I'm benched till the doctor gives me the go-ahead; he's got to make sure the metatarsals are healed completely before I can give up these monkey sticks."

Becky waited for Theo to go into English class. Theo carried her books and pushed back the chair for her. For an instant Becky wished she were back at the clinic with other kids who knew what it was to be sick with a disease that could not be cured with aspirin or penicillin.

"We're so glad you're back, Becky," Carmela squealed. "We missed you so much."

"Hairline fracture, I'm benched for a while," Becky murmured.

"Talk about freak accidents," Rusty sighed. "And during the first season I ever made a varsity team. I suppose if God wanted me to play basketball I would have been born with a basket growing out the top of my head."

"Or a basketball in your stomach," Theo giggled.

Becky glared at her twin. Laughing mindlessly. I'd better not count on her, Becky thought dismally. She watched Rusty swing down the aisle on her crutches to the applause of the other kids in the class. She had a momentary impulse to scrawl *I've got cancer* on the board. She was amazed they accepted her fracture explanation so readily. Of course, why should they think I have cancer; I never think when a kid says she has a broken arm or cramps or strep throat, she's covering up a tumor. Becky opened her notebook. I could handle all of this if I weren't afraid of everybody finding out. If only Sally Beth was here. No way! Jay and Theo will come through for me. They're my real friends. What does Sally Beth care? She just gets off on scaring the new ones. Will Jay be scared when I tell him?

As Mr. Leggett called the class to order, Becky was surprised that he didn't say how glad he was that she was back. The kids settled down and opened their books as though she had nothing more exciting than a twisted ankle.

"What, then, Theo, is the tragedy of *Ethan Frome*?"

"That all three lives are ruined because of that one sleigh ride. Because of the accident they are all drawn together."

"Anyone else care to add? Any more thoughts about what makes tragedy?" Mr. Leggett looked around the classroom. "Can tragic destiny be averted?"

Becky looked at the faces around her, smiling, looking out the window. Vacuous know-nothings, she thought angrily. As suddenly as the anger had frothed, it dissipated. I'm not giving them enough credit. Healthy people don't think about cancer, especially when they are seventeen. Who wants to talk about it anyway? Sally Beth made me crazy with all her talk.

"Did you have time to read the novella, Becky? Do you have any thoughts?"

She paused for a minute. The classroom was silent as a tomb. "The barrier between health and accident, between being well and having a dreadful disease, is much thinner than any of us realize."

Mr. Leggett nodded and said softly, "Ordinarily people are older than you before they realize the truth of that statement. I guess your accident has given you a new perspective. Even that cloud has a silver lining," he finished smoothly.

"Oily bastard," Theo muttered under her breath. Even in English class there's going to be a shadow. Glancing across the aisle at her sister, she felt the weight of the drastic turn their lives had taken.

While Becky was at the hospital, Theo could almost forget the damn tumor. She had attended a Drama Club meeting instead of basketball practice. Becky hated acting but Theo had secretly wanted to be in a play for two years. Closing *Ethan Frome* Theo vowed not to try out for the Senior Play. She must not have fun while Becky couldn't. *Destiny*, she wrote across the cover of the novel. She underlined it and drew daisies around the word for the rest of the English class.

"Look at my hair, it looks like cactus." Becky threw her hairbrush on the bed. "Can I wear your Irish sweater, Theo?"

"You look fine. Don't be so wired. He's going to be overjoyed you're back. He loves you," Theo said earnestly. There was fright in Becky's eyes. Her cheeks were flushed and the hollow in her throat rippled every time she swallowed.

"What time is it?"

"Seven-three. One minute later than it was when you asked me at seven-two."

"I never thought about kids dying," Becky said, "until I was in the clinic."

"Becky, for God's sake. Nobody can handle that trip. What you have can be cured, that's what you have to concentrate on."

"I can't help what I think."

"Don't run that death-downer game. Jay will run out of here faster than crap through a goose."

Becky laughed. "OK, so give Jay the goose!"

"Now let's do the Maitland cakewalk and get you down the stairs. I don't suppose the doctor outlawed a little kissy-kissy in the living room."

"Didn't even mention it," said Becky. "Boy, I can't wait to see him!"

When she was settled on the couch, she held Theo's hand for a moment. "Can you keep Dad and the boys occupied while Jay's here?"

"Absolutely. No one will get within twenty feet of this room except over my dead body."

"Don't say dead body, Theo. It's such a *down*, Theo."

"Glad to see you're learning." Theo grinned. The doorbell rang. "I'll let loverlips in and quietly fade away."

Becky leaned back and pressed her icy fingertips against her flaming cheeks. "Hi, honey," she said, her eyes glowing. "Boy, have I missed you!"

"Oh, Becky." Jay sat beside her. He kissed her

gently, frowning slightly. Becky sighed and held him tightly. He kissed her eyelids and bent to her breasts.

After a few minutes he looked up.

"You're OK? You look OK." He pulled away from her grasp. "I thought you'd be off the crutches by now. I mean it's more than a week."

"Well the doctor wants to be cautious, you know, make sure the leg doesn't get more screwed up."

"What exactly is a hairline fracture?"

Becky's stomach heaved. "I don't know." She reached up to pull him down beside her. He kissed her shoulder and her neck.

"I've missed you so much," he whispered into her hair. He stretched out alongside her. He put his hand on her right leg. "What the hell are you wearing, a chastity belt?"

"A brace," she said, her heart quickening.

"Like a cast?"

"Like a brace."

"You didn't mention a brace."

He moved his hand slowly up her leg, his fingers gliding along the metal up to her thigh. "Becky, it goes all the way up—"

She covered his hand with hers. "It doesn't matter, Jay."

He sat up. "You should have told me."

"What difference does it make?"

"But I thought—you said an *ankle* fracture," he stammered. "Why is the brace up there, so *far*—"

She placed his hand on her left thigh. "There's still one in working order, honey."

"Stop it, Becky. That horrid thing, as though you're strapped inside it." He shuddered and turned away.

Becky's head was spinning. "You know what the brace is bracing?" She was standing outside herself observing herself and Jay. She could hear her words before she uttered them. She was rushing headlong into the scene.

"Becky, maybe I should go. All the hassle you've been through, it's too soon. Why don't we wait till the weekend, the brace will be off then, right?" He smiled nervously.

"The brace isn't coming off," she said, her voice changing tone, like a record whose speed is altered.

"OK, next week then. Our love is strong enough to wait a week," he said soothingly.

"What about a year, what about two years?" Her voice was jumping crazily. "Underneath the love is fear, Jay. Just like the brace is underneath my pants. I can *feel* your fear."

"What do you want from me? You're braced like a set of fragile glasses in a shipping crate, for God's sake! You expect me to be delighted?"

"You don't know the half of it."

"Maybe you'd better tell me." He felt his own anger rising. "Why the brace, Becky?"

Suddenly she became inspired. "Jay, remember when we went camping last summer and my sneakers got soaked in the thunderstorm and I had to slog around cold and miserable?"

[68]

"Wet feet caused this brace thing?"

"No. Remember you told me to think about a bear, whose wet fur got warm and thick in the sun. All morning you made me concentrate on the bear. And soon from toasting my sneakers in the sun my feet actually felt warm and *furry*." Her eyes welled up with tears. "And you kissed my toes because I had felt so miserable in wet sneakers."

"You were one sorry mess! Who leaves their sneakers outside the tent at night but my Becky? Everybody knows you cover your clothes with a tarp." He kissed her nose. "But I was right. The sneakers dried before noon."

"I need you this time because it's a thousand times worse than wet sneakers. It's not a fracture, I have a tumor, Jay."

"A tumor! A tumor!"

"A tumor."

"You mean a tumor, like cancer?"

"Yes. On my leg, right about here, on the bone."

"How could you get a tumor?"

Becky saw her future in Jay's eyes.

"The doctors can cure it. They have these new drugs, the Kennedy kid goes skiing."

"How could it happen? Why you?" She watched him edge across the room until he was out of reach. She wanted to touch him, but her clumsiness with the crutches would certainly make him flee.

"My grandma had cancer. She smelled funny. Her voice was slurred. Her hands looked yellow like chicken feet. I still remember that smell. I tell myself

she was kind, she always fixed cocoa for me, but—"
He fled, slamming the door behind him.

Becky sniffed her hands. "I don't smell," she
sobbed, her grief rising in her throat.

Theo had been waiting in their room, fiddling with
her math notebook, tuning the radio from station
to station. She felt as though an electric current were
passing through her. She could not imagine the scene
in the living room except for Jay's assurance to Becky
that the tumor had nothing to do with *them*.

This scene cheered Theo sufficiently to unwind.
She sat at her desk and began her trig problems.
After Becky told him, they'd probably curse that
they were not alone. Theo wondered how much the
brace would slow them down. Then she stretched
happily. If anyone could work around the damn
brace it would be Becky.

"Theo, Theo, where are you?"

It was Becky. It was only nine-thirty.

Theo raced down the stairs. "Where's Jay?"

"Gone. He probably won't choose medicine as a
career," Becky said, picking at the fabric on the
couch. "I told him, very low key, no heavy number—
all he heard was the word tumor."

"Did you tell him you'd be cured?"

Becky started to cry. "He said cancer. He said cancer and stood up and backed away as though I was
a time bomb." Becky's whole body shook.

"Goddamn yellow-bellied wimp."

Theo held Becky's trembling body and felt her sister's tears soak into her shirt. "Becky, don't. He's not worth it." Theo rubbed her sister's back.

"Becky, Becky! Listen." Theo cleared her throat. "May a hundred thousand sand fleas nest in his armpits," she shouted.

"Shut up, damn it, Theo, I love him." Becky took the ring off her thumb. "He didn't even wait for his ring."

Mrs. Maitland stood in the doorway, afraid of her own violent rage. She wanted to chase Jay down with her car.

"I didn't think I'd have to give up Jay as well as everything else, Mama," Becky said wistfully.

Theo thought of the upcoming Christmas dance, Becky at home, and Jay spreading his oily charm around some eager girls. The enormity of Becky's situation hit Theo full force. She felt defeated too. No more tennis doubles, no cross-country running, no biking, no dancing. Becky couldn't climb into the bleachers, no more sitting upstairs in the movies, no more sliding down the hill to the lake, no more Maitland twins leading the pack. Kids would no longer envy Becky.

"I wish I was back in the hospital, Mama."

"Don't say that, Becky." Theo's voice was loud and tough. "You have to give up sports. Big damn deal. We'll probably both get into a good school, at least Miss Quennell thinks we're a shoo-in at all the colleges we're applying to. We'll study like grinds and cinch places for ourselves. Think of all the millions of things people do sitting down. If everybody played basketball the world would be *boring*."

"I've almost forgotten about college. I'll be fine by then. No crutches or brace." Becky stopped. "Is Jay going to tell everybody 'Becky has cancer'?"

"I doubt it, darling. What can he say? 'Becky is sick so I split'? He'll be sure not to show himself as a heel," her mother said, her face set grimly.

"He might come back, maybe he'll change his mind," Becky said. She leaned against her mother's chest and sobbed.

If she were younger, she'd need me more, Maggie thought. "We all love you so much, darlin'," she repeated again and again.

Theo hurried home to start dinner. Her mother and Becky were going to the clinic every day this week for chemo. The boys were waiting for Theo on the front porch, stamping their feet in the chill. "I hate Mom not being home," Robin said.

"Sorry I'm late."

"When will Becky be back?" Robin asked her.

"Shut up," Mickey snapped.

"What's biting you, Mick?"

"Nothing." Mickey tossed his jacket onto the coat rack.

"This is her long week. They won't get home tonight till you guys are asleep. Like last night. But you can see Becky in the morning."

"When's Dad coming home?" Robin studied her face as if it were a movie screen.

"Usual time, he's at work," Theo said patiently. "Why don't you guys set the table?" She grimaced at the heartiness in her voice. If anyone had spoken that way to her she would have wanted to strangle them, which explained Mickey's murderous look.

"When will they know if Becky's OK?" Robin asked, moving out of Mickey's punching range.

"Jackass!" Mickey moved toward him.

"But it's been so long." He appealed to Theo. "Do *you* know?"

"I wish I did. If I find out anything, I'll tell you," she said, wondering if her parents' decision not to tell the boys about the impending surgery was fair. Give them Christmas, her mother had said, they're so young. Theo balked at scaling down the real facts. A little operation! A lifetime of limping! But she must not think about it. As though Becky might overhear her sister's wretched thoughts.

Such a thin line between caring and sounding like a ghoul, Theo thought, relieved the boys had taken their quarrel into the TV room. I want her to explain why one of the kids at the clinic needs so many blood transfusions but I hate hearing about the tubes and needles and artificial legs. Yet when the kids at school ask how Becky's fracture is healing, I want to yell it's cancer, that's why I look so green and why Becky is dragging her ass between those crutches. If it were a mere fracture, do you think

[73]

I would snap at Rusty or either of us would refuse to watch the team playing basketball? I see them avoiding Becky. Why can't they give us a course in school, while we're still little kids, about diseases and artificial legs so we don't cringe when we come up against them?

Theo took some frozen French fries from the freezer and slammed the box against the counter. Damn cancer—she slammed the box again—damn the treatment and damn the clinic for being so far away, and damn me for bungling every conversation with Becky. Stupid jerk, some great twin for not knowing what to say to make Becky feel better.

She washed the lettuce and made a salad and thought about Jay walking into chem lab with his arm around Carmela. As soon as he saw Theo glaring at him, he jerked his arm away from Carmela as though she were a hot stove. He has a right to date Carmela, Theo thought, and if he had broken up with Becky for any other reason, Theo would simply have written him off. But deserting Becky the way he did. How Theo longed to show him up in front of all the kids. But how to do that without telling them Becky has cancer?

That put Theo back at square one, no closer to figuring out a course of action to lighten Becky's load.

Part Two

Five

Becky had stopped wanting to describe to Theo the contradiction of lying in that small shaded room, four kids getting chemo in four beds, four mini-TV's playing different soaps and game shows, four mothers knitting or snacking to pass the time. One small room. Becky could touch the kid in the next bed and yet each was isolated from the others.

The soft talk mixed with the game-show applause lulled her to sleep. She'd doze off, her arm weighed down by the paraphernalia of the IV equipment, and wake up stiff and sore from lying in one position. When she opened her eyes her mother would spring out of her chair and offer juice, water, did she need the basin to get sick? Poor Mother! She looked apologetic each time she left Becky to have a cigarette in the Parents' Lounge. She smokes and I have cancer, Becky thought when her mother scrabbled in her knitting bag for cigarettes.

Becky hadn't gotten to know any of the other patients beyond the how-you-doing? phase. She envied the little kids their artless hellos and ability to crayon pictures in spite of the drugs dripping into their veins. Of course their casualness resulted from their ignorance, from never having heard the word cancer.

Some of them knew in spite of their parents' vigilance. It had taken Becky ten hours of hospital life to realize these limp kids pale as eggs were many times sicker than the adults would have them believe. But knowing that did not mean she wanted to talk about it. What was there to say? Each week her anger grew. She almost tripped the watery-eyed old bat who passed out balloons and lollipops without ever looking into the faces of the kids. She planned revenge against the social worker who pulled her chair close to Becky's bed and stared greedily at her leg. It's OK to feel anger, she told Becky slyly, waiting to dupe the girl into extravagant confidences. Cancer will cure me of politeness, Becky thought grimly. One day I'm going to tell this bird to get her own disease, and stop feeding off mine.

It's *my* tumor, Becky caught herself thinking, nobody's business but my own. She resisted her parents' determined optimism. She tried to make her mother cry. Some days she wished the doctors would rip off her leg and be done with it. She admired José, a dark lean boy who sprinted down the corridor past all the kids lined up for blood tests, his crutches eating up space. He never wore his prosthetic leg to the hospital; his mocking eyes told Becky he knew his pinned-up pant leg caused the mothers to cluck about his courage, relieved that he wasn't their son.

"That's not going to happen to you," her mother whispered as José shot past them. "You're having the implant, you'll have two legs." One works and the other doesn't, Becky thought. Today she and José had been assigned adjoining beds in the clinic. As soon as Mrs. Maitland departed for her first cigarette, he rolled on his side to face Becky. "Who doin' your operation?"

"Titelbaum. The implant."

"He was supposed to do it on me but it spread, so they had to take the leg. You know you get healed quicker if they cut your leg than if you got gall bladder?"

Becky laughed. "How come you're still getting chemo?"

"They be chasin' that fucker all over my body, they be tellin' me they got to take a piece off the lung next week. McNally, he goin' to do the lung, but I don't know, sometimes I think I'm like one of those animals caught in a trap, you understand? Like I gotta chew off my own leg to get free, 'cause each time they say they be finished, it's always somethin' else, you know what I mean?"

"Do I ever! My folks go on about how lucky I

am Titelbaum does this operation—he invented it, you know—you'll be able to keep your leg, Becky, and I want to ask them, How is a metal bone 'keeping my leg'?"

"They want you to look like everybody else on the outside, don't matter what be doin' on the inside."

Their laughter set their glass bottles tinkling against their metal poles. José turned suddenly and closed his eyes. A social worker was approaching his bed, whispering *José amigo, mira!* He possumed until she tiptoed out of the room. Becky chuckled. Their eyelids were their only protection from curious observers. She felt warm and happy for the first time in weeks.

"How could I enjoy the Christmas dance if Becky is at home, feeling beat by the drugs?"

Freddy crossed his leg over Theo's. "We have to go to the dance; I'm on the committee. You were too. You can't quit everything like you did the basketball team."

"Becky was the better player. They didn't need me."

"We've been through this before, Theo." Freddy frowned. "You were always the better player; Becky practiced harder and had more flashy opportunities playing center."

"Becky is a better athlete," Theo insisted.

Freddy leaned over and kissed her. "Our last

Christmas dance. We aren't going to cure Becky by becoming martyrs. She's had a lousy break—"

"If going to the dance is more important than my sister—" Theo's voice quavered.

"We can't stop living because of Becky."

"You'd better go home, Freddy. I am not going, you know why? Because if I was the one who had it, Becky wouldn't consider going."

"I wouldn't rat out like Jay did."

Theo smiled. "I know, Freddy. Go to the dance. Have a good time, honest, I won't be mad. I have to stay with Becky." Theo's voice sounded artificial in her own ears. Freddy rolled his eyes.

"Without you? That will be swell fun. Now that we've got it out in the open I have been a bloody saint through all this. And you are mad because I want to spend one night, our Christmas *dance* for God's sake, alone with you—" He kicked the table leg.

"We'll have plenty of time alone when Becky's in the hospital." Theo covered her face with her hands. "Oh my God!" she cried and ran from the room. At the door she paused for an instant, then ran out into the night.

She ran two blocks before the frigid wind penetrated her misery. Hunching her shoulders against the cold she crept onto the back porch and waited for Freddy to leave. She understood for the first time that what made these spates of anger and pain so bottomless was that there was no one to blame.

The house was unnaturally quiet. Theo called to her brothers. Becky probably had heard as much of Theo's outburst as they had.

The boys came to the top of the stairs. Robin hesitated a few steps behind Mickey.

"Stop looking as though you've witnessed mass murder," Theo snapped.

"What did he do?" Robin asked.

"Nothing. We had a fight. It's been building up for a long time." Theo spoke airily and waved her hands.

"You seemed to like him well enough on the couch last Sunday night." Mickey smiled slyly.

"There is no privacy in this place." Theo was glad for the chance to be righteous.

"If I wanted to make out with a girl, I would choose a more secret place than the living room," Mickey told her.

"You're full of opinions, Mickey." Theo narrowed her eyes. She didn't have the energy to carry it any further.

Becky was on a new drug; she had been sick all night. Two more rounds of chemo, then she would be off the hook till the surgery in January. They had to build up her body and her blood counts, try to repair what the chemo had destroyed so she would be healthy enough for surgery.

Word about Becky's tumor had seeped out. Rusty had whispered to Theo, "We are all so sorry about Becky. We won't say anything."

"You've already said too much." Theo flung the words at Rusty with such force, most of the girls avoided her more than Becky. But Theo didn't care about their increasing coolness to her.

When Becky had returned to school after the second round of chemo, Theo was stunned that there were no plans for a big party in Becky's honor. She suggested it to Freddy and Rusty. Both of them looked embarrassed. "We don't need you, we don't need any of you," Theo growled. "Some swell friends, talk about loyalty."

"We'll give her the biggest party in the world, if she gets better," Rusty blurted out.

Now Theo cried if the bathwater wasn't hot enough or if the boys wanted to watch a TV show she didn't want to watch. Her tears made her parents angry. "Why are *you* crying?" they asked. Theo would race to her room and muffle her tears in her pillow. If Becky was in the room, Theo would hide in the bathroom, feeling hunted.

"The hell with the other kids," Theo told Becky, "we don't need them."

"It's harder for you, seeing them at school every day." Becky yawned. "My real friends are at the clinic."

"I am so glad I gave up the team. I never realized how much time we wasted running up and down that gym. We're lucky to be out of all that razzle."

Becky smiled and reached for Theo's hand. "Oh, we're lucky all right."

In the mornings while Theo helped her dress and made both their beds Becky would think of the sacrifice Theo was making. But before she could thank her twin an inner voice snarled, Some sacrifice, she can run over to Freddy's whenever she chooses, no tumor growing inside her.

Theo had said she wanted to go to the clinic, but Becky saw the revulsion on Theo's face when Becky told her about José's stump. Theo's clumsy attempts to hide her feelings goaded Becky into peppering her conversation with statements such as "Sally Beth told me three kids croaked last week but I stopped counting. Most of them will be dead by spring."

Theo's hands trembled. Her eyes were dark holes.

Sometimes when she was alone in the house Theo locked her leg stiff. After a few minutes she grew impatient dragging the leg. Some nights she'd wake up suddenly. Lying in the darkness she'd wonder, Why Becky, why not me? She tried not to compare Becky's cancer with her own health but she couldn't avoid the sense of being overpowered by the will of God. Or was it the caprice of luck?

Mickey tugged at Theo's arm. "Have we seen the last of Freddy? Do you hate him?"

"Leave me alone. I'd like to see the last of you."

"Excuse me for living. I'm going to talk to Becky. She doesn't bite my head off."

"Buzz off, Mickey." Theo shoved him aside and slammed the door to her room behind her.

"Guess what, Beck? I finally got the guts to tell Freddy to vanish!"

"What a lousy liar you are!"

"Can't be good at everything," Theo said sharply.

Becky closed her book. "You going to the dance?"

Theo sat on the foot of Becky's bed. "No way. And don't give me any lectures about how I should go and have fun for both of us. I've made up my mind."

"I'm glad you're not going. Why should I watch you get dressed and float out of here?"

"Couldn't you go? The doctor didn't say you have to stay home."

Becky made a fist. "He didn't say watching a bunch of kids have fun would cure my cancer either. I'm tired of being brave. I envy the little kids; they yowl their heads off at the clinic. What do they know; it's all just needles to them."

"Stop, Becky, please." Theo clapped her hands over her ears.

Becky sighed. "At the clinic some mothers act so stupid. One fool won't let her daughter be in a bed next to a boy. And the kid is only about nine. 'This room for girls only,' her mother says in a fake high-pitched voice. 'You boys go to the blue room next door.' Last week she made a sign, LITTLE GIRLS' SUGAR AND SPICE ROOM. Mom and I howled."

Everything leads back to the clinic, Theo thought. She put on her nightgown and brushed her hair.

"I may try out for Drama Club. They're doing

[85]

The Boy Friend as the Spring Play. I think it sounds like fun, dancing the Charleston."

"Do you have to carry on about dancing?" Becky snapped.

"Sorry." Theo sighed.

"When Mom and I were driving into the clinic the other day she told me about her rotten year."

"Her rotten year?" Theo rummaged in her bureau drawer. "Do you have a nail file I could use?"

"In the john, third shelf, medicine cabinet."

Theo opened the cabinet filled with rows of pill bottles from the hospital. The labels didn't say what the pills were for or how frequently they should be taken. Theo never asked what each bottle was for.

"What about Mom?" Theo asked, returning with the nail file.

"When she was a Senior she had expected to be class secretary and tennis varsity captain. She didn't get either one. Plus the guy she liked dropped her and started dating the girl next door. Mom didn't have a single date her whole Senior year."

"Poor Mom," Theo said vaguely. She wondered if Becky's arsenal of pills was for the pain or to knock out the tumor.

"Yeah. Her biggest problem was that she ate herself into a size sixteen and hated herself." Becky's eyes narrowed. "The moral of the story was that someday I'll think of Jay as a passing piece of scum."

"Of course you will. And you can tell your daughter about what a swine Jay what's-his-name was."

"A boy at the clinic told me the drugs make you sterile."

"How does he know?"

"He's been sick almost two years. He's having his sperm frozen."

"Yuck. I wouldn't want to ask for ice at his house."

"Theo! Gross!"

"Well, how does he know you will be sterile?"

"Sally Beth's afraid to have kids because they'll be deformed from the radiation."

"Sally Beth's fifteen. She'd better be afraid to have kids. Why don't you ask Titelbaum?"

"Sure, Theo. Can't you see Mom's face when I say 'Thanks for this fancy new leg, Doc, now when can I have kids? Will they all be born with tumors in their legs?' "

"Cut it out, Becky."

"There's this girl Margaret who has leukemia. She's seventeen and she was in complete remission for three years. Now she's relapsed and they are bombarding her with experimental drugs. First she lost her eyebrows and eyelashes and then with last week's dose she lost her pubic hair. For Margaret that was the final straw. She's begging her folks to let her go off the drug. It may never grow back."

Theo exploded with laughter. "What a wild clinic! Can't I come with you next time?"

"We don't find it quite the chuckle you do." Becky's face had frozen.

Theo threw herself down on the bed. Becky

watched her cry for several minutes. "Stop, Theo. I'm sorry. I get high and mighty like Sally Beth sometimes, thinking the tumor gives me the right to shoot everybody down. Really I am sorry."

Theo lifted her face and wiped her eyes on her sleeve. "How come you have a little hair—I mean on your head. Is it OK to say that? Don't get mad."

"One of the nurses warned me. I'll be shiny bald before Christmas. Mom says she'll buy me a wig but I think it's dumb."

"No, it's fabulous. Get a long blond one. Oh, Becky!"

"What are you crying for?" Becky was losing control again.

Plump tears rained down Theo's cheeks. "If you get a blond wig, we won't look like twins anymore."

"If I'm bald we won't look alike either."

Theo opened her bureau and snatched up a pair of scissors. She clipped a hunk of hair from above her left ear. "We'll still look alike, damn it, nobody's going to take our twinning away, not even the great Dr. Titelbaum."

"You're crazy. Put those scissors down. One of us bald is plenty. I'll wear a scarf or my Yankee cap. Come on Theo, don't cry. My hair'll grow back."

"Then mine will too." Theo snipped hair from over her right ear. "Are they even?"

"Come here, you look like a clown—" Becky tried to rearrange the tufts of hair protruding from the sides of Theo's head. "Maybe Mom'll buy you a wig."

"What are you girls laughing over?" Mrs. Maitland stood in the doorway, her face pink from the cold night air.

"Look at Theo's hair," Becky said, falling back against her pillows, laughing fitfully.

"Theo, what have you done!"

"Well, Becky's going to be bald—"

"Mom, can we have a Christmas party?" Becky swung her legs to the floor and stood next to her mother. "Please, a whopping big party? With Robin as Santa?"

"It's a marvelous idea."

"Will my hair grow by then?" Theo asked, tugging at her hair with a mournful expression. "When will I learn to think?"

"Never, you always were the dumb one, maybe you didn't get enough oxygen in the womb." Becky and her mother laughed.

"When should we have the party? Christmas Eve?" Theo asked.

"No, I like our family ritual with lamb for dinner and church."

"Day after Christmas. Everybody's really dragged out then."

"OK, day after Christmas it is. Let's tell Daddy." Mrs. Maitland went to the hall to call her husband.

"What's all the commotion up here?" he asked as he ran up the stairs. "Becky OK? Don't tell me Freddy went home without being asked?"

"Don't you notice anything weird about Theo's

hair, Daddy?" Becky leaned back against the wall, feeling the warmth of her family around her.

"No. Looks the same to me." He walked around Theo peering at her hair. "Did you curl it?"

Sunday afternoon Becky was still basking in the feeling of well-being she had gained after talking with Theo. Teasing her brothers and shouting tips to them as they stumbled around the yard trying to catch the football their father was throwing, Becky realized how much she had missed doing daily things with the boys. She had been so focused on her own problem she had deprived herself of the family fun she loved.

Theo was sorting laundry with her mother. "I had an awful fight with Freddy. Do you think I should go to the dance?"

"I don't think Becky would want you to stay home on her account."

"Wrong. I told her I wasn't going and she was glad. She doesn't want to watch me get dressed and all."

"Theo, you can't stop your life because of Becky's tumor."

"That's what Freddy says. But how can I try out for the Spring Play when I see Becky struggling down the hall to class?"

"That's natural, feeling guilty. I've gone over every minute of Becky's life to see where she got this tumor. I called Dr. Truscott to find out how many dental X rays Becky's had since she was five!"

"Really, Mom?"

"And cigarettes, and pollution from the oil refineries when we used to live in Millburn, and even if I took any drugs when I was carrying you two. And yes, my darling, I even get terrified in the night that you may end up with one too."

"So do I, Mom. I wake up, my skin crawling, wondering why Becky and not me. Mom, how could God let kids get cancer?"

Mrs. Maitland hugged her daughter and shook her head. "You're thinking in human terms, God had a greater design, I suppose. One of the mothers at the clinic says God only gives it to kids who can handle it."

Theo turned toward the window, where Becky was showing the boys how to position their hands to catch the football. "Becky is handling it because she has no choice."

"But some of those little kids, Theo, they are so gutsy—" Mrs. Maitland folded the last towel and picked up the stack of clean laundry.

"Should I call Freddy, won't it be horribly selfish?"

"I don't know anymore what is selfish. This whole business has stretched all my Momisms out of shape."

"You're doing great, Mom. If you weren't so calm, Becky might panic. You make it all seem so ordinary. Go to the clinic, barf a few times—even the brace, and going up and down stairs."

"You should see me backstage, before the performance. But Becky makes it easy for me. Dad and I had planned for hours, for days, how to tell her about the surgery. Driving into clinic one morning she said, 'Mom, am I having Titelbaum's implant or the other?' Calm as a cat after a meal.

"I should have credited the kids' grapevine. They know more about pain and endurance, oh Lord, more about faith and courage than any of us. They pass on information to each other out of the sides of their mouths like convicts in Clint Eastwood movies. The only thing they don't know about is which kids don't make it."

Theo saw that her mother wanted to believe the kids didn't know about death. So she said nothing. Each week Becky went through a litany about who had died, mostly kids Becky had never met at the clinic. Theo knew she kept scrupulous records of the remissions and the relapses as well.

"We are certainly lucky Titelbaum caught it so early. We have so much to be thankful for. Becky will get well. Call Freddy."

"What if Becky gets mad?"

"She'll have to work that out for herself."

Six

By nine-thirty in the morning Mercy Hospital Children's Clinic looks like a war zone. The clinic occupies an entire floor of the world-famous medical center. It is a city block square. The clinic sees more than one hundred children a day. There are about one thousand active patients, who come to the clinic for primary treatment for various types of cancer.

There are also children on maintenance doses of medication. They only have monthly appointments. The maintenance kids are the glamour people, whispered about by the newcomers because the monthly kids have already been through the surgery and chemo or radiation. They've reached the halfway mark: they are in remission, a state longed for like Nirvana. It means the patient is free of the cancer. No one speaks of cure, but long-term remission, one, two, three years without the cancer returning, is the state everyone prays for. Kids who have survived six or seven years are legends.

Occasionally one of the legends will come back to the clinic to visit, the way some people return to schools they've attended. Usually they return because they're going off to college or are getting married. One came back because he had played on a winning hockey team in college after most of the doctors in town had given up on him.

It's a good ritual, returning and thumbing your nose at cancer. It's what keeps the kids lining up for their chemo, week after week, each one planning how he'll come back and walk the halls in victory.

Along one long corridor parents and children wait for routine blood tests before their appointments with one of the doctors, who will decide whether bone scans, X rays, transfusions, or other lab tests are indicated. Parents of young children are the most nervous. During their first week at the clinic, Mrs. Maitland had caught herself thanking God that it was Becky and not Robin. She thought of his pale-freckled nose and was relieved she didn't have to lie to him. It was difficult enough never saying cancer or tumor in front of him or Mickey, but if Robin had been the patient, she would have been as hollow and fidgeting as the mothers trying to distract their small children from the sights and sounds of the clinic. The parents looked as frightened as their children when the receptionist announced their names and treatment-room numbers over the loud-speaker.

On the other side of the floor is a long string of rooms where the children receive chemo or sleep after bone-marrow infusions and spinal taps, procedures after which they must lie immobile for an hour. This area is referred to as the day hospital; it is filled to capacity by ten-thirty, so the children with late appointments have to spend the day in the corridors, lying on stretchers with their chemo bottles swinging high over their heads; their vomit basins and bed-pans in plain view of everyone who passes through the clinic.

There has been an attempt to put the adolescent patients in the three or four rooms farthest from the nurses' station, an acknowledgment that they need more privacy than the little kids.

Today Becky was assigned to room 6. She hoped José would be there. She looked forward to seeing the boy, who took his cancer without a drop of self-pity. It gave her a shot of confidence to watch him manipulate so well around beds, IV poles, other patients. Balancing on a crutch he looked like a long golden stork. When he slept, his head totally devoid of hair looked like a carving of polished wood.

As she entered the room, Becky saw that she was the first.

"You get your choice of beds this morning, Becky." The nurse spoke brightly.

"The window," Becky said immediately. "Could you put José in here please?"

"He won't be coming today," the nurse told her.

"Yes he is. We're on the same schedule."

"Not anymore," the nurse said casually, as she tied a rubber tourniquet around Becky's upper arm.

"What's happened to him, oh that's right, he's having lung surgery, so he's on the ward, right?"

"Make a fist. You've got good veins, Becky." The nurse attached the tubing and strapped Becky's forearm to a board so the needle wouldn't dislodge itself from her vein.

"Where's José!" Becky twisted to a sitting position.

"Don't get yourself upset, dear." Mrs. Maitland settled into the hard chair to the left of her daughter's bed. "Oh, damn, I forgot my book." She looked around the room, hoping someone had left a magazine behind. But today the place was spotless, the sheets crisp and wrinkleless. She could not concentrate on Becky's conversation with the IV nurse. All she could think of was six hours with nothing to read. She had vowed never to sink into the TV abyss.

"Do you mind if I go to the shop downstairs, Becky? I forgot my book."

"Mom, they won't tell me anything about José."

"Now darling, it's probably medical ethics or a hospital rule. After all José has a right to privacy."

Becky looked at her mother perched on the chair like a bird on a telephone wire, waiting to fly off. "Go downstairs."

"Do you want anything?"

"Just go, Mom." Becky waited until the nurse and her mother had left the room, then she picked up the metal bedpan and flung it against the wall. Three nurses came running into the room.

"Will someone tell me where José is? The surgery went OK, didn't it?"

The nurses conferred and Miss Bishop, the head nurse, approached Becky's bed. She adjusted the IV equipment so that the liquid would drip more quickly into Becky's vein. "Hey, slow it down," Becky said irritably. "It burns when it drips that fast." She turned her back, wondering how she could penetrate their smug secrecy to find out about José.

"I didn't make it too fast, Becky, it was barely running. Remember, you've got to drink a lot today."

"Please tell me why José isn't here."

"I'm not supposed to do this, Becky, but I'll give you José's phone number."

"Then he's home? He's OK?"

"Would you like to talk to Miss Walker?"

Becky rolled over and looked at the gray-haired woman, whose skin was as pale and tight as the sheets on the three empty beds. "I don't need a social worker, I need a telephone."

"Oh, you can't call from here," Miss Bishop said nervously. "Now you relax. Want me to turn on the TV?"

"No. Thank you."

Another kid was wheeled into the room. She

looked like a large doll in the huge stretcher with its metal sidebars raised. "Make them stop, Mommy, make them go away. It hurts, Mommy," she repeated until Becky thought she'd go mad. The child's mother looked like a child herself, her eyes wide and frightened. Miss Bishop went to the child.

"Now Kathy, you've been through this so many times, you're always my best patient. What's the matter this morning?"

"Take it out, it burns, my arm hurts, they did it wrong!" The child dragged out each word; her voice was harsh and flat.

"Would you like some juice?" Miss Bishop asked.

Kathy screamed. Her mother apologized to the nurse and smiled at Becky. "I don't know what's wrong with her today."

"How about a toy from the Playroom, Kathy?" Miss Bishop asked. "Or a puzzle?"

"Mommy!" Kathy screamed. "Mommy, help me!"

Another child was wheeled in. Becky sat up to see if she knew the girl, she seemed to be asleep. Becky didn't recognize her.

"They'll be hanging two units of blood in a few minutes. Her father's in the Blood Bank giving platelets, she's very low," the nurse told Miss Bishop across Becky's bed.

Another stretcher was wheeled in. "We're all here," Becky thought grimly. The boy stared at the ceiling, humming a tuneless song. There was no adult with him. Becky touched Miss Bishop's arm as the

[98]

nurses were leaving the room. "Please don't forget about José's number?"

"I won't, dear. See if you can talk to Kathy. It's not good for her to be so upset." Miss Bishop went over to the sleeping girl and wrote something on a long piece of adhesive tape, which she stuck to the siderails.

"OK, Kathy," she said loudly over the child's screams, which were as regular as the ticking of a clock. "No more or the doctor'll make you stay overnight. We only have good children here in the clinic. You don't want another needle, do you?"

Kathy's mother followed Miss Bishop from the room. "Hey, Kathy, maybe they'll give your Mom a needle," Becky called to her.

Kathy stopped screaming as suddenly as if someone had pulled a plug from its socket. "I don't think so," she said, frowning.

"Good morning, children." A pink-cheeked woman in a yellow volunteer pinafore came into the room wheeling a cart of books, tiny dolls, crayons and balloons. She took a stack of paper and held it up. "Who wants to draw?" she asked with a gleaming smile.

"I do, give me paper," Kathy growled.

"What about you, dear?" the woman asked Becky.

"Kathy's going to draw me a picture, aren't you, Kathy?"

"Give me crayons," she said, not looking at the woman. "Not those, I need new ones, with points."

"Let me see, do we have new crayons for Kathy?"

The girl across from Becky woke up and clapped her hand over her mouth. Her mother, who had been sitting silently, wearing a black shapeless coat, jumped up to get her a basin. Neither Becky nor Kathy were disturbed by the girl's heaving.

"If she'd give me some good crayons I'd draw you a picture," Kathy said loudly. "I'd draw you a Mickey."

"I have a brother named Mickey." Becky sat up and leaned toward Kathy. The child's scarf had slipped back on her bald head. When she smiled she had a dimple. She dropped her eyes shyly.

"I don't have any brothers or sisters."

"I have a twin named Theo."

"Does she look like you?"

"Sure does." Becky pointed to her own head. She had a few wisps of hair and she had not yet lost her eyebrows. "Except she's not bald."

Kathy laughed and for the first time sounded like a little girl. "Mine grew in for school, then I had to get more medicine and it fell out again. Now I can't go to school till after Christmas. My mom got me a wig; it's black; it has bangs and no curls."

"I don't have a wig. I wear a baseball cap."

Kathy's mother came back into the room. "Are you OK, do you want to get sick, honey, do you need to pee?"

"I want a baseball cap, I don't want the wig."

"OK, we'll get you a baseball cap. You said you wanted the wig, you picked it out."

"Well, I changed my mind," she said, her voice hoarse.

"Get me something to lean on, you should have brought my crayons, these have no good points. I want to make Becky a picture."

Kathy's mother was almost in tears. "You said you didn't want your crayons, Daddy asked you this morning."

"I want them now, I want to make Becky a picture."

"I'm back, Becky love." Mrs. Maitland held up an armful of magazines.

The mother of the silent girl stood up. "Maggie, I brought you the pattern for the sweater you admired last week."

Becky hadn't thought the mothers formed friendships while their children slept. Her mother looked capable and relaxed. Kathy's mother was wringing her hands. Becky wondered if she ever behaved tyrannically toward her mother the way Kathy did. Becky felt a strong rush of affection for her mother—never complaining although Becky's tumor had separated her from the well-ordered routine of her life, had isolated her from her friends as much as it had Becky. All this time she had been so wrapped up in her own feelings she had thought nothing of her mother. She reached for Maggie's hand and squeezed it. She would tell her on the way home how grateful she was that she had never left her on her own to cope with the hospital. José's mother didn't spend her days sitting by her son's bed, nor did Sally Beth's. Only about half the teenagers had mothers like Maggie, who stayed with their children every minute. José had told her that little kids whose mothers worked got relatives to bring them. If they had no relatives, the hospital assigned someone to accompany them to the hospital and paid them government money. Ironically José's mother had been one of the "transportation" women before he'd gotten sick. That's why she had brought him to the clinic even though it was two hours' subway from their house. Becky suspected he was too *macho* to admit to his mama that he wanted her around. Becky had never had to ask her mother.

"I can't draw Mickey without a good red for his pants," Kathy snapped to her mother. "A red with a point."

"I'm glad you're here, Ma," Becky whispered with tears in her eyes. Embarrassed, she turned away and tried to block out the sounds of the clinic.

"Here's your first unit of blood, Cindy," a nurse called. Becky noted that she swished her hips as though she were a bar waitress. She's only a couple years older than I am, Becky thought. The nurse took Cindy's full basin and returned with a paper cup with mouthwash. Becky curled up and caught her mother's attention. "No way I'd ever be a nurse."

"Me either," her mother answered strongly.

It was after nine-thirty that night when Becky and her mother pulled into the driveway. Theo came hurtling out the door and ran to the car. "Wait till you see the beard I made Robin. He's going to break a lot of hearts as Santa. What a ham he is! He's been ho-hoing since he got home from school."

"Take these things into the house, Theo. Hand your sister her crutches. And what are you doing out here without a coat?"

"Take it easy, Mom. You guys hungry? I kept the stew hot."

"Gross!" Becky sighed. "I just want to go to bed."

She leaned against Theo and swung up onto the crutches. "Help me get upstairs, Theo. I'm not going to eat, Mom," she called over her shoulder. "So don't bother fixing me a tray."

"I was hoping somebody would fix *me* a tray." Maggie closed the garage door and followed her daughters into the house. She watched the girls inching their way up the stairs. She went into the living room where her husband was stretched out on the couch, sipping a glass of Scotch and watching a basketball game. He grunted a hello. "Becky OK?" he murmured.

"Don't bother getting up to look."

He shot to his feet. "What's the matter?"

"I have been driving four hours today. It took me a half hour to find a garage to leave the car. And you're watching TV!"

"Would you be happier if I sat in the dark?"

"I'd be happier if you'd go to the hospital once in a while."

"I have to work every day."

"You could take a day."

"I wouldn't know what to do if Becky got sick in the car."

"You pull over and wait," his wife said.

"I'm no good in hospitals."

"Nobody is."

"All right, I'll take her next time."

Theo came into the room. "Becky's really shot. I could barely get her into bed. What'd they do to her today?"

"Cytoxan. She didn't go to sleep, did she? She's got to drink at least twenty-four ounces tonight to flush out the drug. Oh, she'll be furious if I wake her." She threw a challenging look to her husband.

"OK, I'll handle it. How many ounces?"

"Just make her drink a glass of juice and one of water. Then write down what she drinks on this sheet." She handed him a folded piece of paper from her purse. "Theo, be a love and fix me a tall Scotch and water." She collapsed onto the couch.

"Can we talk about the party?" Theo asked, turning the sound down on the TV.

"Sure," her mother said drowsily. "Ho, ho, ho, ho."

Becky woke early. She knew she had to do something important but she couldn't remember what it was. Theo was a long lump, her head burrowed under the covers. Becky had always envied the way her sister could sleep through any crisis. Becky would lie awake watching the patterns of tossing trees on the ceiling. Theo three minutes after turning off the lights was asleep and slept soundly until the alarm yanked her awake the following morning. When Becky was on methotrexate she slept that way— dreamless, sleep coming suddenly and completely.

The sense of urgency that had shaken Becky awake this morning had become fairly common since she had been diagnosed. She had a new mental calendar—the first day, the morning she had been told about the tumor; the second day, when she knew the tumor was malignant; the third day, the beginning of chemo. Her next red-letter day would be going in for the surgery, then the six weeks of lying immobile in bed waiting for her body to accept the metal bone, then more chemo, then finally, like the Christmas on a yearly calendar, remission—return to being Becky—then the calendar could be discarded. She would be ready for a new year.

Some mornings she woke thinking of Jay, wishing today would be the day he would approach her at school, insist they talk privately and take her in his arms and confess how foolish he had been. These dreams gave Becky such pain she tried to banish them. Jay smiled at her in the halls, he still sat next to her in English class and asked solicitously about her leg. He never referred to it in words—just a gesture toward the stiffly braced leg. "How is it?" he asked and remarked every day that she was the bravest person he knew.

I'm not brave, I'd love to unscrew it, leave it at the hospital, get a brand-new real live human leg with no tumor, and run onto the basketball court knowing you will be waiting for me every day. I'd give anything to put back time to the day before the tumor, I'd love to outrun the damn thing. *Brave?* I don't have any choice. I have to let them pump me full of drugs, perform all their tricks to outsmart the tumor.

Becky would reach a point in this imaginary monologue when she became so angry her leg became separate from the rest of her body. She thought about sticking pins into it, lighting matches at the site of her tumor. She would pinch her right thigh until tears stood in her eyes. Damn Jay for refusing to touch her now. She wanted to tell him it was the same leg that had excited him last summer on the beach.

She remembered why she was awake. She had to call José. The alarm rang; Theo's arm snaked out from the covers and hit the radio.

"Be careful, you almost knocked over the lamp," Becky said.

Theo's head appeared. "God, who set the alarm? It's Saturday. We can sleep."

"Sorry. I was afraid I'd sleep too late. Would you do me a big favor? Get my purse from downstairs?"

"Now? It's eight o'clock!"

"It's important."

"Are you going to be sick? Do you need Mom?"

Theo was up and across the room instantly. "What's the matter?"

"I have to call this guy."

"You have to call a guy!" Theo socked herself on the head. "You have to call a guy now? What guy? He work the night shift?"

"Maybe. I don't know. He's from the hospital. José. He was supposed to have lung surgery but none of the nurses will tell me why he wasn't at the clinic yesterday."

"OK, you have to wake up this José and his family because he didn't show at clinic?"

"I was afraid he might have, well, you know."

"You mean—" Theo gestured.

"Dead," Becky answered.

"Maybe he had a cold or maybe he overslept. He doesn't have to be . . . just because he didn't appear."

"Lots of kids *disappear*. The nurses say they went home, or they're off treatment, but we know what it means."

"You're going to be fine, Becky."

"Some of them won't be."

"What's wrong with José?"

"Osteo like me. But his has metastasized into his lungs." Becky's voice was flat. Theo was unable to intuit her feelings.

"He makes me laugh even when I'm retching from chemo," Becky continued. "He told me about a little boy about four or five years old. He was screaming his head off while he was on the ward. The doctor told him if he didn't stop screaming the doctor would make him leave the hospital." Becky's face creased into a broad grin. "So the kid waited until midnight, got out of bed, got his clothes and got dressed and got all the way to the lobby before a guard stopped him. The kid explained to the guard, 'They said if I didn't stop yelling I'd have to leave, so I am leaving.'"

Theo didn't think it was a funny story. "Does it hurt a lot, the drugs and needles?"

Becky shrugged, unable to describe the dread that had become her constant shadow. "I have pills for leg pain but I have stopped taking them. The pain will be worse after the surgery and I don't want to be pilled out."

"Those pills in the john! I was afraid to ask."

"Ask me anything, Theo, if I don't want to talk, I'll tell you. I'm so used to little kids like Kathy, who's learned to draw with whichever hand isn't taped to an IV board. If you saw some of the kids at the clinic, you'd panic."

"I'm not that shallow," Theo said hotly.

"I've been afraid from the beginning that I'd end up crippled, nobody wanting to look at me, but it's not something you talk about. If it happens, it happens."

Theo didn't recognize Becky for a moment. Unable to stand seeing her twin as an unknown person, she rushed to Becky and collapsed against her. "Tell me everything, please, so it won't separate us."

"You have to think about whether you want to come to the hospital after my surgery. You're going to be scared and want to run when you see kids who look like concentration camp victims—it's impossible to forget."

"Is there a lot of pain?"

"Nobody talks about it. If you see a kid sleeping all day, it's not a good sign. If a kid in the clinic falls asleep leaning against the wall or with his head on his shoulder, he is feeling punk. It's never spelled out."

How could she explain to Theo. The hospital was a different world! To the doctors Becky was an interesting osteo, to the nurses a girl who didn't complain and was easy to handle. To José she was a girl who was lucky to be getting the implant, and back in Maplewood she was repulsive to Jay, devastating to her parents, fascinating to the kids at school, who had never seen a kid with cancer. Often she dreamed of climbing mountains, unable to get a solid foothold. In her dreams she had two normal legs; she ran perfectly while she slept and woke suddenly when she stumbled and fell.

Theo was exhausted. How many times did she have to tell Becky that she would go through it, fifty-fifty, the perfect loyal twin. What would convince Becky? "Some days I envy Mom," Theo said. "I wish I knew all the kids you talk about, the nurses, even the layout of the place. I want to know who José is so I don't make jerky jokes about him. I won't run, Becky." She paused. "At least I hope not."

"Get my bag, ace. Let's find out what José is doing."

"He's probably sleeping," Theo grumbled. She found the bag and sat on the bottom step. She could never be as strong as Becky. Talk about guts! Each time Theo guided Becky's immobile leg, she prayed she wouldn't bang it into the wall or the stairs. Helping Becky off with her clothes she tried not to touch the skin of the bad leg. Theo always took a shower after helping Becky get settled for the night. Everybody laughed when Mickey asked if Becky's sickness was catching. Theo was not completely reassured by their parents' answers. After all, what did any of them know about cancer?

"Hey Theo, what's going on down there?"

"Just wanted to give José a few more minutes to sleep."

"Hello, is José there?"

"Just a minutes," a woman's heavily accented voice answered.

"Yeah," a sleepy voice came on the phone.

"José, hi, it's Becky Maitland, sorry I woke you."

"Who's this?" The voice sounded suspicious.

"Becky Maitland."

"Say what?"

"Becky from the hospital."

"Becky, oh Becky, what's happenin'?"

"That's what I want to know. You weren't at the clinic, I was getting chemo yesterday and they wouldn't tell me where you were," she said, her words rushing together.

"Well, thas nice, you callin' me. Thas real nice. But I'll tell you what's goin' down. I decided no more chemo, no more cuttin'. I had enough."

"But you have to. Without the chemo, you might—"

"Croak? Shit, I'm going to get offed anyway. Make no nevermind if they slow it up with motherfuckin' drugs."

"You're going to be OK, José, with chemo, and you gotta let McNally do your lung."

"Listen, I turned eighteen last week. I say what I do from now on, not those doctors or my mother."

"What does she want you to do? What about your father?"

"He split after my brother was blown away in Nam."

"Oh. What about your mother?"

"She be cryin' and all, but I promised I'd see Sister Rita Divine, this healer Mama know. So she ain't too uptight. She know those drugs killin' me anyway. Just a little slower, thas all it mean."

Becky was crying. "No it's not true, talk to the doctors," she sobbed. "Please come back, please, please José."

"Hey, you be cryin' because I won't take them drugs?"

"I'm not crying, please, at least talk to Titelbaum."

"Told him I didn't want him to have me cut again. He said it was up to me, he said he got a waitin' list, kids wantin' to be cut, he not waitin' for José Malingua to get his act together."

Becky realized she had never heard his last name. She didn't even know where José lived. All she knew about him was that he was letting the damn cancer choke out his lungs. "Could I call you next week, to find out how you're getting on?" she asked softly.

"Thas real nice. No one from the hospital ever call me before, except that Miss Walker, who tell me I gotta right to be angry but that don't mean I gotta right to go off chemo."

"She's right, and I never thought I'd agree with that simp, but you gotta give the drugs a chance."

"I been on them, Becky baby, for two years. I got enough scars on me to pass for a POW. When you goin' in, anyhow?"

"Second of January."

"Maybe I'll come visit you."

"Would you! I'd like that!"

"Take care, honey, you was real nice to call, I mean it. Say, where you callin' from?"

"I live in Maplewood, New Jersey."

"That's where Bobby from. You know what he call Jersey—cancer alley! You never knew him, he was before your time."

Becky wouldn't ask where Bobby was now. "Please come back."

"OK, I'll think about it," he said. " 'Bye, baby."

"One thing we got to do today is get presents for the boys. Any ideas?" Theo asked Becky after breakfast.

"We can get Robin one of those mechanical ray guns he keeps talking about, the kind that flashes red and green."

"Mom doesn't approve." Theo knelt and hooked the brace around Becky's shoe and snapped it into place.

"He plays with them at other kids' houses, so it amounts to the same thing. What about Mom and Dad? You want to go in on something together?"

Theo looked up. "Us together or them together?"

"Us. We could get something fluffy, she always says she hates house things for *her* Christmas present. We could get her one of those bath oil, powder sets."

"What about Dad? *The New Yorker* subscription again?"

"It's tradition, we have to," Becky chuckled. "He depends on us. Remember how we used to get him Old Spice when we were little. For his birthday, Father's Day, Christmas, even Thanksgiving one year? I felt like the world collapsed one day when I opened his cabinet and saw all those unused bottles. I was so sure he loved it, that it was the best present in the world, and here they were, lined up as proof that I didn't understand anything about him."

"Really? When you showed me those bottles I

thought finally we can get him something else. He's got enough shaving lotion for his whole life. It was as though we were getting him a present for the first time instead of that automatic 'Oh we have to remember his Old Spice.'" Theo picked up her purse and her sister's. "You want anything else? I'll take these down and come back for you. Mom said she's willing to drive us to the shopping center and pick us up but she doesn't have time to shop today. You know, she looks like hell."

"Because of me and the hospital?" Becky asked sharply.

"Come on, Becky. She looks like hell."

"And it's my fault?"

"Can't anyone have pain except you anymore? Can't any of us feel down?"

"Sorry. She does look lousy. She sits in the hospital and makes an effort with the other mothers. I see her trying to look interested and be polite, even with Mrs. Romagnola. That woman waddles over to us and pretends to whisper to Mom and talks loud enough for everyone to hear, 'Mollie is very bad. I talked to her mother yesterday, her white count is so high they can't do nothin'. I hope I hear in time to go to the wake.'"

"Oh, Jesus! They say stuff like that?"

"Not Mom. But some do and they pretend we can't hear them. They never say directly to a kid that another kid is going, or has gone. But they talk about it around us, and we never admit we hear.

It's an unspoken rule, like not bragging about a good blood count or asking where a patient is. That's why I got so crazy about José. Not knowing gets me panicked."

"We should do something special for Mom. What about a special dinner for her and Dad, private with candles and we keep the boys down in the TV room so Mom and Dad can have a romantic time," Becky said.

"While we're out let's buy a steak for them. As a surprise." Theo glowed. "Be back in a minute." She headed downstairs with the crutches.

Becky doubted they could afford a steak but she was touched by Theo's immediate generosity. Her twin was usually kinder and more alert to other people's feelings.

Theo bounded up the stairs. "OK, ready. Mom's backing out the car. Dad's picking up some wine, I told him about the surprise and he gave me ten bucks so we can buy them a steak a foot thick."

"I was wondering how we could buy Christmas presents and a steak."

"What about we get Mickey a Superman T-shirt because he's been really super this fall?" Becky eased herself down the first flight of stairs backward, leaning on the banister and supporting herself with her right hand on the top step. "He's been doing laundry—not that it takes a genius to run the washing machine. Helping with the housework is his way of helping with my leg, you know?"

"I could never get through all this if you weren't so super, Becky."

"Me! I'm the lucky one having you," Becky said.

"Imagine having to buy that Mrs. Romagnola a Christmas present."

Becky giggled. "A muzzle."

Seven

"Do all the gingerbread men have to be Santa?" Robin asked.

"Of course, it's Christmas, fool," Mickey told him.

"They're your men, make 'em whatever you want," Becky said. She was decorating orange-spice Christmas trees.

"Mickey's made enough Santas for six trees." She winked at Mickey before he had a chance to object.

"Becky, love, look what the mailman delivered," Mrs. Maitland handed her daughter a large stiff envelope about twelve inches square. Her name and address were printed with Magic Markers in a rainbow of colors.

"Wonder who sent it, there's no return address," Becky mused. "Get me some scissors, Mick." Becky snipped at the tape reinforcing the edges of the envelope. "It's from José. It's a huge Christmas card he made himself."

The painting showed the Holy Family and worshipers around the Christ Child. The Holy Child was lying on a hospital bed instead of a pile of straw. The people surrounding him were doctors and nurses in white uniforms, two children in wheelchairs and a tall bald young man with one leg, leaning on a pair of crutches.

"Mom, this boy, looking down at the Child! It's José." Becky leaned forward excitedly. "This little girl in the chair must be Kathy." Becky pointed to the figure holding a Mickey Mouse toy out to the Child on the bed. The Blessed Virgin bore a striking resemblance to Mrs. Romagnola. Instead of gentle animals surrounding the Child, complicated-looking hospital equipment had been painted lurid silver.

The picture was entitled "Waiting for Johnny Miracle."

"What does it mean?" Robin asked. "Why are the doctors looking at Baby Jesus?"

Mickey was clearly impressed. "Wish I could paint like that."

"José thought about this scene a long time," Mrs. Maitland said softly.

"He's really talented, isn't he, Mom?" Becky asked. She looked for her own face in the picture and was disappointed he hadn't included her. "He never told me he was an artist."

"He's *very* talented. Someday . . . we should have this framed," Mrs. Maitland said.

[118]

Thinking *someday* filled her with a resounding sense of loss. It was painful to nurture José's talent or dream about feisty little Kathy's future. The only way to survive each round of treatment, each setback and even each good sign, was to live only for today, scurry from the dreams of maybe he'll be an artist, or design engines, or she might want to hitchhike through Holland. Must never dwell on the fact that many of the children would never live in their own homes or hold their own children.

"Now, Mickey," Maggie said briskly, "we want the tree up and the cookies finished before Grandma and Grandpa Maitland get here."

"Grandma's going to get weepy when she sees me, isn't she?" Becky said. "Know what she told Theo on the phone last week? She'd cut off both her legs if it would help me," Becky said nastily.

"Grandma's weird," Robin said. "How could her legs make a difference to Becky?" He took a hunk of raw cookie batter and stuffed it into his mouth. "Oh, Mom, it tastes awful."

"Well, you finish it, greedy piggy," Becky told him.

"Hi, guys." Theo staggered into the kitchen, her arms filled with dusty cardboard boxes. "Look what I have!"

"The lights, it's the lights," Robin said, running to his sister, leaving a knife full of red frosting lying on his gingerbread cookie. "Can I help with the lights?"

"What about the cookies?" Becky said, laughing.

"Mickey's done enough for six trees," he said gleefully. "Come on Theo, I know how to test them, we have to plug them in before we hang them."

"Hey, Mick, go see how Dad's coming with the tree," Becky said, wanting a moment alone to study José's painting.

There was a knock at the kitchen door. Becky looked up and there was Jay walking toward her.

"Making cookies?" he asked, pointing to the table crowded with cookie sheets and bowls of green and red frosting.

"Lucky guess," Becky said, cringing at the nervousness in her voice. "Grab a knife. I need all the help I can get."

"No thanks, I don't have time. Got to get the car back."

Becky felt embarrassed for him. His eyes flicked around the room but the cupboards and sink and refrigerator offered him no help. Hey diddle diddle Jay wants to jump over the moon. And the dish ran away with the spoon. His coming to see her was a good sign.

"I brought you this present, it's not much."

Becky reached for the package. "I'll put it under the tree."

"Carmela told me you'd be in the hospital so I thought—"

"Carmela?" Becky had rehearsed a reunion with Jay countless times. She knew of course that Carmela had moved in on Jay as soon as he was free. Lying in the clinic Becky thought of vicious zingers about

Carmela, but surrounded by cookie dough in the Maitlands' kitchen she could think of nothing clever.

Jay looked embarrassed. "I guess you've heard."

"I didn't expect you to join a monastery," Becky snapped.

"I'll never forget you, Becky," he said.

"I haven't died," she said.

"I didn't mean that, *oh*, I get sick at the thought of that tumor. I still care about you as a person."

"Have a merry Christmas," Becky said, her voice grating harshly. She took the wrapped package and flung it at the door. "And give your present to Carmela."

Jay shook his head and nudged the package with his toe across the floor close to where Becky was sitting. He opened the door and shrugged. "I shouldn't have come."

"The box is not contaminated, Jay. Tumors aren't contagious."

He said nothing. Just closed the door gently behind him.

And the dish ran away from the spoon.

"Becky's crying, Mom, she's not frosting cookies, she's in here crying," Robin shouted as he ran through the kitchen, his hands full of dead Christmas-tree lights.

"Darling, what is it? Do you feel sick?" Mrs. Maitland looked at her daughter weeping, her head drooping onto her chest.

"Jay came over. He wouldn't even touch me," Becky sobbed. She kicked over the chair her right leg had been propped on. "It's not fair."

"Jay's a jackass, honey, afraid to face up to things."

Theo came in with tinsel hanging from her ears. "Meet Theo, your mobile Christmas tree. What's the matter, Becky?"

"Apparently Jay came over and upset her."

"That jerk here? Is this from him?" Theo bent toward the package. "At least it isn't ticking."

Becky laughed through her tears.

"Maybe it's a Carmela doll. Wind it up and it grabs second-hand boyfriends." Theo ripped open the package as she spoke. "Look, Becky, it's two little bears cuddling each other. They are dear even if they are from him."

She held out the furry brown bears to her sister.

"I don't want any part of his guilt numbers." Becky pushed herself away from the table. "Hand me my crutches, Theo. I'll supervise the tree."

"Good idea. Mickey'll hang all the red ornaments in one place and all the blue crowded onto another. Come on, Mom," Theo gestured to her mother. "You can hang the high ones with me." She turned back toward Becky. "Dad's sulking because he wanted a table tree."

"Same routine every Christmas," Mrs. Maitland sighed. " 'Let's have plenty of kids,' he said the first year we were married, 'so they can help you with the Christmas tree.' "

"As good a reason as any," Becky said. "Let's wrap up those bears and give them to Kathy at the hospital, Mom."

"Her mother said Kathy would probably be spending Christmas on the ward; she had been so hoping to have this Christmas at home. They were on the ward last Christmas and Kathy's birthday too."

"You know, when I asked her for her address, she gave me the hospital," Becky said.

It was barely light when Becky and her mother got to the clinic the following morning. Seven A.M., and a concrete pall hung over the city. Even the hospital security guards and elevator starters looked sleepy. When they got to the clinic, Becky was surprised to see a line of patients already waiting for blood tests.

"The motto of this place could be 'We never sleep. Mercy twenty-four hours a day,' " Mrs. Maitland murmured to Becky. "Want some coffee or juice— I bet the coffee shop isn't open yet, but maybe one of the aides could sneak some in from the cafeteria."

"No thanks. I'm better getting chemo on an empty stomach, less to throw up."

"But you haven't been drinking enough. Dr. Greene is going to have a fit, you heard him, you must flush the drugs out of your healthy tissue by drinking, what about some Hawaiian Punch?" Mrs. Maitland said, in a perfect imitation of the volunteer who pushed a cart of sweet drinks around the clinic.

Becky was stunned by the display of dusty plastic poinsettias and sprigs of dark-green holly, with jagged plastic tips. Massive gold-foil stars hung from the ceiling every ten or fifteen feet. A silver Christmas tree stood in front of the nurses' station—its tiny pinlights winking spasmodically.

The spindly-legged children waiting for the doctors looked out of place. The frenzied setting called for rosy-cheeked cherubs caroling cheerfully, not fretful babies wailing in their mothers' arms.

"Let's see if Kathy's scheduled today," Mrs. Maitland said. Becky looked at the slips the nurse had handed her.

"I'm down for a chest X ray," Becky sighed. "We'll be here all day. Don't you think they could tell us in advance?"

"We could give Kathy the bears," Mrs. Maitland said quickly. She hoped Becky wasn't going to complain all day.

"Hey, Becky Maitland, how you doin'?"

"Sally Beth!"

The girl wheeled over to Becky's bench. "Early bird gets the sharp needles," she said cheerfully.

Sally Beth looked pale and too thin. Her skin was chalky. "I have early chemo. One of my cousins drove me. You'd think they could schedule us at human hours. We had to leave home at five goddamn thirty."

She swears to get a rise out of me. I am not biting, Maggie thought. "I'm going down to search for coffee, OK, Becky?"

"Sure."

Maggie walked away unnoticed.

"I shouldn't bitch today. I am much better, Becky. Bet my counts are in normal range today."

Becky agreed. Privately she thought the odds were slim. All the starch seemed to have gone from Sally Beth. She drooped in the chair. When she talked she sounded breathless.

"Mariela Romagnola's back in. On the ward. What luck that kid has. She's in for an infection, and her counts are so low, they're falling off the page. They're trying to juice her up on blood and antibiotics but it's the pits."

"What's happening with you?" Becky asked.

"Mom's got off till New Year's. We're going to go shopping, get me some new clothes. And one of my dear friends is having a disco skating party, and she didn't invite me."

"My loyal sister is going to a Christmas dance tonight." Becky was losing control. She had never spoken her anger at Theo. She willed her voice back to its normal range. "Think you'll go back to school after New Year's?"

"I quit last month. Who needs that aggravation? The home tutor practically dipped her pencils in Lysol."

"That's one advantage to Theo. She's helping me with my assignments. But school stinks. Some of my teachers would prefer a leper in class."

Maggie Maitland rejoined the girls. "Nothing's opened yet."

Sally Beth turned toward her. "So your other daughter's going to a dance tonight. That's nice."

Maggie glared at Becky. "Theo agonized over going to that dance. What would you have her do?"

"Nothing, Mom. She made the choice. That's all we're saying."

"Try to have a little feeling for the rest of us."

"OK, Mom, I hear you." Becky rolled her eyes. "Where are the chemo nurses anyway? We're on time and they could care less."

"When you coming in for the big event?" Sally Beth asked.

"Day after New Year's."

"You'll love that, Mrs. M. Mothers got to be up and dressed by seven-thirty."

Becky laughed. "Poor Mom!" But her face showed no sympathy.

"You can thank Mrs. Romagnola for that. She's famous around here. She's got to weigh three hundred—"

"I know her," Mrs. Maitland said coldly. "A lovely woman."

"Well, she has this red see-through nightgown that she wears when Mariela is on the ward. She sticks to that kid like glue. She won't leave her alone for an hour! Anyway one morning an intern comes in, early rounds, and there's Mrs. R., groggy, in her tiny cot. She sees the doctor and leaps up, these immense boobs hanging out to here."

Becky was doubled over laughing. Mrs. Maitland

felt like an abbess. But she was helpless to punish either girl.

"Anyway," Sally Beth continued, "they passed this rule about boobs out of sight by seven-thirty. They say that intern quit medicine."

Mrs. Maitland flounced down the hall to have a cigarette.

Evergreen boughs lined the aisles and candles were flickering in gleaming silver holders at the entrance to each pew. The altar was massed with red poinsettias and a spotlight fell on the figures of the Holy Family in their familiar crèche nestled on a bed of straw. Clay and paper animals made by the Sunday-school classes were placed in the straw watching the miracle of Christmas unfold. The children's choir waited restlessly in the first three pews, swinging their legs in time to the carols being played on the organ. Christmas Eve service was always well attended, perhaps because the children had such a large part in the festivities.

Reverend Goode, Bible in hand, looked out over his holiday congregation. "It is a time for joy and a time for rejoicing, it is a time for renewing ourselves and our pledge to Christ, it is a time for giving gifts to one another as symbols of the Greatest Gift our world has ever received. Our Lord gave us His Only Begotten Son, on Christmas Day. Let us pray in joy and in thanks to Our Father saying as His Son taught us, Our Father who art in Heaven . . ."

Becky wondered if José still went to church. She had heard tales from Sally Beth of the old priest who was so afraid of the sick kids on the ward that he closed his eyes while bringing them Communion. She looked at her mother, hands covering her eyes. She's praying for me, Becky thought, so are Theo and Daddy. She looked at Robin sitting between his parents trying to catch the attention of several friends in the choir. Mickey sat at the end of the pew ahead of them, fiddling with the red scarf tied over his white choir robe.

". . . and let us ask Him to guard and protect Becky Maitland and her family in this time of great trial."

Becky felt her face grow hot. How could he! In front of the whole congregation! Her mother leaned over and squeezed one hand and Theo squeezed the other.

Mickey stood up and walked down the aisle and out the back door of the church. A few people turned to watch him. Mrs. Maitland gasped. "Oh, Dick, do something!" she whispered.

Mr. Maitland followed his son, conscious of everyone watching him. Mickey was in a corner hugging the wall. As his father approached he could see the boy crying, his fists striking the wainscoting.

"Mickey, Reverend Goode was saying what he thought would help us. He was asking everyone to pray for Becky."

"Why? They only pray for people who are going to die!"

Mr. Maitland turned his son around to face him. "That's not so, Mickey. You know that Becky has something wrong with her leg. The doctors have given her lots of medicine, that's why she goes into the hospital every week, right?" The boy nodded.

Mr. Maitland wiped the tears from Mickey's cheeks. Kneeling in front of his son, he tried to find the right words. "The doctors think Becky is going to need an operation, because there is something wrong with the bone in her right leg that the medicine can't fix. We didn't tell you about the operation, we thought we would wait till after Christmas—"

"Does Becky know?"

"Yes, honey, Becky and Theo both know. And so does Reverend Goode. That's why he was asking everyone to pray. Mom and I pray, and we would like you to pray for Becky. Because she will have to stay in the hospital for about six weeks and Mom will stay with her. So we have to pray that we can all get through this tough time. It will be hard for us as a family—maybe we should have told you, after all, you are involved, too. Will you pray for Becky, Mickey?"

"I hate God. Why doesn't he do it to those kids who mug people and set fires?"

"I don't know, son. Maybe you should ask Reverend Goode. Don't be angry that he asked everyone to pray for us.

"Becky has the best doctors in the world, the surgeon, the one who's going to fix her leg, well he's like the Reggie Jackson of doctors. He's going to bat a thousand with our Becky, you wait and see."

"You swear, you *swear* she'll be all right?" Mickey said, looking into his father's eyes.

"I can't promise that. But I can promise that we will all do everything in our power to help Becky. That's why we found this super doctor—he invented the operation."

"When does she go for the operation?"

"After New Year's. Grandma Maitland will stay with us and Mom will stay with Becky."

"What about you?"

"I'll be running back and forth like a runner hung up between bases."

Mickey frowned. "Don't make jokes, not about Becky, not in church," Mickey said. "Don't say anything to Robin. He's too young to understand. He's afraid of doctors. Can we ask God to promise Becky will be all right?"

"Every day, ace."

"I'm sorry I ran out, Dad. But I still don't understand why God would do this to Becky when there are so many crummy kids he could have done it to instead."

"I don't know either, Mickey. Maybe we'll understand someday."

"I don't care if I never understand as long as Becky gets well. Let's go back in, it's almost time for us to sing."

As Mickey slipped into the choir pew, the choirmaster gave the signal and all the singers stood. Robin leaned over and whispered to his mother, "Is

Mickey in trouble? Is Dad mad?"

"No, I am not mad," his father whispered. "Mickey had to go to the john, now be quiet and pay attention."

Maggie Maitland winked at her husband and sat back to enjoy the Christmas carols. Whatever had transpired, Mickey was singing in full voice with the glimmer of a smile on his face.

"I still wish he hadn't made a public announcement; it made me feel like one of those Care poster children," Becky muttered.

Robin in the front seat of the car, between his parents, heard none of the conversation in the backseat. Mickey leaned over and patted Becky's shoulder. "Dad explained everything to me and I prayed to God to keep an eye on you," he whispered in her ear, "when you're in the hospital. Dad and I don't think Robin should know yet, so be cool."

Becky leaned toward her brother, and kissed his nose. "With both you and God, I never had it so good. Thanks, Mick."

"What's all that whispering?" Mr. Maitland said. "I bet Grandma and Grandpa Maitland will be at the house when we get home."

Theo caught Becky's glance. "I hope she's calm, Dad, last week on the phone she sounded like a diva in the last act of *Bohème*, 'Nothing surprises me anymore; we've all been too lucky too long,' she says."

"Now Theo, she's your grandmother," her father began.

"Was she always like that, thinking that the line is longest when she's on it, or that the bakery sells out of rolls just because she's having a party and is desperate for rolls?"

"Let's say she had leanings, but as she's got older, she's fallen into that world-revolves-around-me trap. But be patient, she loves us all very much, and it's just her way."

"You all talking about Grandma?" Robin asked, much surprised. "I think she's great. She never says things like 'when I was your age,' the way most old people do."

"Grandma will be delighted to be called an old person," Mrs. Maitland laughed.

"How old is Grandma?" Robin asked.

"Sixty, last year she was sixty," Mickey shouted.

"Sixty, and you say she's not old?" Robin asked his mother.

"This is going to be a swell Christmas," Theo said.

"Can we open presents tonight?" Mickey asked, seeing the jovial mood of his parents.

"No of course not," his father answered.

"Well, maybe one each, but just one," his mother said.

"Wait till you see what I got you, Theo," Robin sang.

"I did see it, you showed me last week," she laughed.

"This is a good time for me to give Becky a present," Theo continued.

"Where is it? I don't see it!" Robin shouted.

"Becky is the present," Theo said. "To Maplewood High!" She had rehearsed this speech several times.

"Whatever are you talking about?"

"You, Becky. I got the idea watching you teach the boys how to throw the football. Coach Hawkins agreed. When you get sprung from the hospital, you'll be the assistant coach of the baseball team, and if you can spare the time from making up chem labs"—Theo was bouncing with excitement—"you can coach track and field—boys as well as girls."

Dick Maitland sounded the horn a few times. "Theo, you're a genius."

"It sure will be good to get back into things. And your vacation's over too, Twin. You're back doing laps," Becky said, her face creased in happiness.

"Me and my big ideas," Theo moaned. If God makes Becky well, I'll drop out of the Drama Club and do laps till I drop. God, let Becky be normal again! I want to be a twin again!

"Now that the little ones are in bed, we can speak freely. It certainly is a strain trying to be cheerful, looking at that poor child's leg stiff in that miserable brace."

Alma Maitland rummaged in her purse for a handkerchief. "There's never been cancer in our family, I can't understand it."

Maggie glowered at her mother-in-law. Dick

glanced from his wife to his mother, who had covered her face with her hands. He went to her and gently took her hands in his.

"Mother, we are not going to dip into self-pity. We don't want Becky to lose her courage, she has a long road ahead and we have to be positive."

Alma looked up at her son. "Well, Dick, we don't have to be positive when the poor child isn't listening. We can at least speak honestly among ourselves. I have some Laetrile that Violet Moss got in Mexico. I have enough for three weeks and if it works Marty and I will fly to Mexico and smuggle in enough for another month, they only let you have thirty-day supplies, apparently."

"Dad, will you please tell Mother that Becky is not taking Laetrile, we do not want you to smuggle drugs, we are following what Dr. Titelbaum prescribes *to the letter*, will you explain that to Mother?" Dick Maitland tried to keep the exasperation out of his voice.

"You know your mother, son."

"Do you have any proof Laetrile doesn't work?" Alma demanded.

"Mother, the answer is *no* to Laetrile and any other quackeries you may have up your sleeve."

"I also have not up my sleeve but in my purse the name of a doctor in Alabama who cures people of cancer by running chemical tests on their spit. Then he puts them on a fast, drinking a special kind of water, until the cancer gets *starved* and shrivels to nothing."

Dick Maitland looked at his wife and shook his head helplessly. "If it weren't so loony, it would be funny."

"Now you listen to me, Dicky, you don't know any more about this cancer business than the next person. Violet's sister was given up for dead, the doctors gave her a month, two at most, and she went to this man in Alabama, stayed at his retreat for thirty days, and that was two years ago. I saw her last week and she is as healthy as you or I. Don't tell *me* what's best for Becky."

"What would it hurt, Maggie, if you gave Becky the Laetrile as well as the drugs the doctors are using?" her father-in-law asked.

"I don't know. But it might make her condition worse."

"Have you asked Titelbaum about Laetrile? Have you mentioned any of the clinics curing people without these poisonous drugs and radiation?"

"Of course I asked him about Laetrile." Maggie lit a cigarette and hastily stubbed it out when she saw she had one burning in the ashtray. "He wouldn't even discuss it. He said 'Mrs. Maitland, I am a busy man. These quacks should be jailed. There is no question that Laetrile and malva flowers and vitamin therapy are all useless. The only way to fight cancer effectively is with the protocol we use here.' " She stood up and leaned against the fireplace. "Then he said if we want to try these other remedies, he can't stop us. But he emphasized—'Do not bring Becky back to the clinic and do not expect me to operate on her.' "

"That's a threat!" her mother-in-law said, for once stunned into silence. She opened her purse and took out a slip of paper. "You keep this in case you change your mind. That doctor of yours sounds like a beast, refusing even to admit other methods can help cancer people."

"Mother, did it ever occur to you he knows more than we do about medicine and doesn't like to see people duped by quacks and hucksters?" Dick asked.

"Violet's sister would not go to a quack!"

"Let's not discuss it. We want the best Christmas ever so Becky's spirits will be high when she goes into the hospital. We all need some fun, it's been a heavy fall."

"Don't I know that, Maggie! It's the grandparents who suffer the most in these cases, nobody remembers the grandparents. It's been a living hell, I tell you."

"I'm sure it has, Mother," Dick said between clenched teeth. "What about a glass of brandy before we turn in? Mickey and Robin will have us up at the crack of dawn!"

"Well, maybe a spot for me, what about you, Alma?"

"Perhaps it will help me sleep. I haven't slept much since we got the news," Alma Maitland sighed and sniffed loudly. "How do you think I feel when my friends are showing pictures of their grandchildren and ask how my marvelous twins are. What can I say?"

Maggie jumped to her feet. "Excuse me," she said hastily and fled the room. She had known Dick's mother was going to be a problem but she hadn't anticipated wanting to choke her a mere three hours after her arrival. Trying to make the tragedy her own. Maggie recalled a conversation with Sam Waters' mother. Sam had been Robin's best friend since nursery school. Now Mrs. Waters would not allow Sam to play at the Maitlands' house.

"You have to understand my point of view, Maggie. Sam is so young. Of course we all know Becky will get well. But if she didn't, God forbid, but if she didn't how would we explain it to Sam? We feel he's too young to have to know about such things."

So many women had written her notes of sympathy, already burying Becky, not allowing a ray of hope to permeate their suggestions for prayer chains, hot baths, lobelia tea, cold baths, a doctor in Massachusetts, a faith healer in New Mexico.

"Who treated the Kennedy boy?" Rusty Wheeler's mother asked Maggie at a PTA meeting. "Maybe he could help Becky too. I am down on my prayer bones more times than I care to tell you, praying my heart out for that little girl. You know those twins of yours are special children, God won't take one without the other, oh I mean he won't take Becky neither, she don't look bad, I always thought people with cancer looked spotty, you know *liverish*."

Maggie Maitland smiled politely and edged away. No wonder Rusty surrounded herself with funny lines and quick wit. That woman's voice was enough to scrape the scales off fish.

Maggie set the kettle on the stove and ran hot water through the teapot. Perhaps a pot of tea would break Alma's poor-me monologue better than brandy. After all, Maggie thought, it can't be easy for Dick to sit there and listen to her carrying on. She measured a few spoonfuls of tea and added a pinch of peppermint leaves. Outsiders didn't understand that the most important thing was to keep a semblance of normalcy. Even though you remembered with every breath that your child had a malignant tumor in her leg, you also had to struggle to remember that life was precious—not just Becky's but all the other children's. From the day Dr. Titelbaum had outlined the course of treatment, Maggie had felt as though she saw and heard everything with sharpened senses. So much of life had become habit before the shock of Becky's illness. Now the windows through which Maggie observed life had been so highly polished that people and animals and cars, even the aides at the clinic sneaking into the Lounge to watch soap operas, all took on a clear precision.

When her mother suggested on the phone that perhaps they should amputate Becky's leg just to be on the safe side, Maggie heard Celeste saying are you certain this doctor and his operation are any good? With Becky sustaining a life-threatening illness, Maggie realized she could no longer nod agreement to her husband's opinions or the thoughts of her family and friends. And she must not squander her energy now on silly arguments with her mother-in-law.

Trying to explain her heightened vigilance to her husband, Maggie had said, "It's as though I am staying awake during a long night waiting for her fever to break. Only the long night is a year."

He hadn't answered immediately. She was grateful for that. It meant he was thinking, not listening with the halfway listening when one is waiting one's turn to speak instead of paying close attention to what the other person is saying.

"I find I want to preach to people," Dick admitted to her a few nights later, "I want to stop people on the street and say, Listen, love your kids and take those family trips you keep postponing. Live for the joy of today; something terrible may happen to rob you of tomorrow. Then I come home and find Mickey's left his bike in the driveway or Theo's left the oven on all night and I forget all that love and bawl them out same as I did before Becky was diagnosed."

"The thing of it is cancer does change your whole life but it doesn't change every day, that's what people can't understand. Becky and I argue in the car going to the clinic; she is ready to die of embarrassment when she's trying to be cool talking to her friend José and I remind her she must drink another glass of juice."

"Just as though we were at the gym at school and I yelled something inappropriate when she was standing at the foul line," Dick added.

Maggie set some mugs on a tray and fixed a plate of sliced fruitcake. This year's batch had very few candied cherries as Theo had eaten most of them straight from the jar. Theo was trying so hard to be an adult during Becky's illness. And Becky is still a seventeen-year-old. Instead of wondering about the hospital's success rate, she hopes José will be in the same room at the clinic. She agonizes over losing Jay, over losing her hair, over losing her spot on the basketball team. She wonders which clothes will best disguise her brace, and trying to be brave, she admits none of it to me.

Part Three

Eight

Theresa Campanile had been a pediatric nurse for five years at Mercy Hospital. During that time she had watched many families check into the ward—frightened children with eyes large as prunes, parents with stricken expressions. There were mothers who had packed everything from portable phonographs to plastic bowls bulging with pasta. There were fathers who rained questions on her like blows, talking fast to cover their panic.

When the Maitlands stepped off the elevator, Theresa assessed them quickly. There was a look of determination on Becky's face as she pointed one of her crutches at Theresa. "I'm going out of here with two legs, all I'm leaving behind is the tumor."

Theresa noticed a bag full of schoolbooks. Becky was not going to cut herself off from school—that other world—the way so many of the kids did. Theresa knew if they kept strong ties, it would be easier for them to bridge the gulf upon leaving the hospital. Some of the patients grew into the habit of thinking of the hospital as security and were reluctant to leave. From the look on Becky's face, Theresa knew she would not be one of them.

"Here's your home, A26, best room in the house," Theresa said. "You can hang your clothes in here, and this is your bathroom—not that you'll be seeing it, Becky."

"Who's my roommate?" Becky asked while she unpacked her books.

"Mariela Romagnola. A very sweet girl."

"Don't you have any guys for me? I might as well have some fun while I'm here."

"Against hospital regulations. Richard and Sally Beth have been trying to room together for two years. As a matter of fact, Richard's in now. Since we have a shortage of male patients he's all alone."

"I was only kidding, Theresa."

"If you had to juggle room assignments you wouldn't think it's funny. We always have too many girls."

"Sounds like our eighth-grade dance. Six boys for about sixteen girls. And in our school we got a lot of man-eaters."

Becky shooed her father out of the room and undressed. As she slipped her arms into the hospital gown and looked down at her bare thighs, she felt repelled. "Mom! Buy me some decent gowns! I can't be so *exposed!*"

Theresa shook her head. "You're going to have to wear it. For the first couple weeks you're going to be flat on your back, we will be rolling you like a log to bathe you and change the bed each day. Matthew, the physical therapist who works with Dr. Titelbaum's patients, will be up in a little while to teach you about the trapeze." The nurse pointed to a triangular piece of metal hung from the top frame of the bed. "Are you ever lucky. Matthew's a dreamboat."

Becky smiled at the antique word.

"We'll be irrigating the wound for the first few days with antibiotics—to prevent infection. When you wake up, you'll see tubes coming out of the wound and you'll have a catheter because the doctor doesn't want you to be lifted even for a bedpan—"

"Enough!" Becky groaned. "I'd rather not know." She looked up and saw a young man with a dazzling smile and curly blond hair; "This place is getting better by the minute," she laughed.

"Hi, I'm Matthew Bell. I'll be working with you after the implant, to teach you how to regain balance, build up your arm muscles. Make sure the hips are aligned properly."

Becky grinned. "Sounds like a car tune-up."

"Dr. Titelbaum is a perfectionist, and he's very possessive about his implants."

Matthew reached over Becky's head to adjust the

trapeze. "Now lie flat—after the surgery, you'll be flat for two weeks—and reach *up* with your arms. Now grasp the metal bar and *lift, lift*—"

Becky blushed as Matthew leaned over her body and gripped her forearms. "That's good, Becky, now lift your upper torso as though you were chinning, up, up, *hold it.*" He laced his large hands around her back to support her. "Remember, you will be raising only the upper part of your body. Your hips and legs must remain motionless."

"It's much easier with you holding me," she chuckled. "I don't have long to practice. If Titelbaum had told me, I could have worked out at home."

"Don't worry. Using the crutches has given you a lot of strength in your shoulders and arms. Your body looks good."

So does yours, Becky thought. She held his gaze, while damning the stupid hospital gown, which had all the charm of a flour sack. "Will you be here a lot?" she asked casually.

"Every day, they work us student therapists to the hilt." He winked at her.

For the rest of the day Becky glowed. Sitting in the bed with nurses and technicians swarming around her, she felt like a celebrity. When two young residents stopped in to wish her good luck in the operating room, her anxiety gave way to a cheerful bravado.

Becky and Theo had shopped for artificial flowers

to decorate Becky's trapeze and posters to hang on the wall alongside her bed. She had brought a stack of paperback novels, a couple of decks of cards, a large can of salted nuts, and of course all her school books. She had pictures of Theo and the boys, a pink squirrel from Rusty, Mickey's lucky Yankee baseball cap, and a portable radio. Waiting in her room at the hospital were a mammoth basket of fresh fruit from Grandma and Grandpa Bacon and an avalanche of cards.

While Becky was opening the cards and taping them to the wall around the bed, Mrs. Maitland hung up her clean blouses and an extra pair of pants in the narrow closet at the foot of Becky's bed. She had stowed their toilet articles in the table and grimaced at the bedpans and gauze dressings in the bathroom. It was going to be strange living in this one room—she and Becky and Mariela and the never-silent Loretta Romagnola. Maggie felt a stab of panic—there was no privacy. She wouldn't have a bed to lie on till the cots were opened after nine o'clock at night. She blanched at the thought of six weeks in that yellow plastic armchair, six weeks of visibility. She glanced at Becky, offering Theresa some grapes. Becky had already decorated the room, made it her own. Maggie marveled at her daughter's composure and resolved to be as brave as Becky in spite of the nagging worries.

"Hi Becky." Mariela waved from the wheelchair. Her mother was puffing along behind her, pushing the chair and talking to one of the residents who was walking next to her.

"My daughter's been here two weeks, and you still haven't found what's causing the infection. What's the matter?"

"Ma, leave him alone, it's not his fault."

"You want to stay here and be their guinea pig or you want to go home?" her mother answered quickly.

"I'm glad we're going to be roommates," Becky said.

"I never roomed with an osteo before, when do they do it?"

"Tuesday morning."

"Who's your doctor?" Loretta Romagnola asked as she rehung Mariela's bottle onto the IV pole next to her bed. "You OK, Mariela?"

"Titelbaum," Becky told her, already beginning to sense the confusion when Mrs. Romagnola was presiding. She looked at one person while she was asking questions of another. Becky glanced furtively at her own mother. Mrs. Maitland was folding Becky's T-shirts to fit into the narrow bedside drawer. Becky suspected her mother would have preferred to fold herself into the drawer.

"He's the best, makes the other cutters look like chopmeat," Mrs. Romagnola said. She sailed across the room and picked up a large brown bag. "You want to eat? Nice hot cinnamon rolls my husband sends up from the bakery every morning, Mariela won't eat the hospital garbage, all she needs to get out of here is to eat, but will she do that? Anything to eat she wants I'll buy her. But then it sits on that table until it's hard like a rock."

"Ma, stop it. I can't eat, it makes me gassy," Mariela whined.

"Gas is from being empty. Fill up your stomach and you won't have gas," Mrs. Romagnola said and tore off a piece of roll with her teeth. While she chewed she nodded her head and poured herself a cup of coffee. "Coffee we have in the room, my Sal brings my coffeepot every time we come in, he knows I can't drink the crap in this place, anytime you want coffee, you help yourself, don't matter if I'm in the room or no."

"Thanks, I could use some coffee," Mrs. Maitland told her. "But you must let me contribute too, I'll buy the next can of coffee, OK?"

"Get out! Sal he brings it from the place, don't worry, you'll give me plenty, it all works itself out." She glanced at her daughter. "Not that we're going to be here long, I told the doctors this morning, they got another four, five days to find this infection, then I'm taking Mariela home. She should stay here while they take their sweet time?"

"How are you feeling, Mariela?" Mrs. Maitland asked.

"There was a little blood in the bedpan this morning," she said.

"It was nothing, *nothing*, I told you." Her mother

[149]

tossed the bag of rolls back into the drawer. "See where I'm putting these, Becky, you want a roll?"

"Thank you, not right now."

"Hello, girls, time for a chest X ray, Becky." Theresa held an order slip in her hand. She motioned Becky into the wheelchair.

"Hey, I can walk," Becky told her.

"Hospital policy, while you're here, you ride."

"That's silly. I can walk!" The wheelchair made the surgery seem very soon.

The elevator doors slid open. A small child was wheeled onto the ward on a stretcher. She was lying on her back moaning softly in her sleep. The orderlies left her in the hall while they danced around with a couple of the aides.

Becky tried to concentrate on her bathrobe. She gazed at the familiar blue and red plaid. She couldn't remember the colors of her brothers' bathrobes.

Theresa braked the chair outside the X-ray department. "One of the orderlies'll bring you back. Do you know Barbara?" she pointed to the little girl in the chair ahead of Becky's.

"Hi Barbara," Becky smiled.

"Hi yourself," Barbara said. "What're you in for?"

"Robbing a bank," Becky said out of the side of her mouth. She was rewarded with a sunny grin.

Barbara held out her arm, palm up. The inside of her forearm was bruised black and blue. "I told Dr. Coale this morning, you got one chance to find the vein, you miss it, you're out of the game."

Becky saw an IV running in the child's other arm.

She was pale, but her vivid blue eyes were shiny, more alert than many of the kids Becky had seen in the clinic or on the ward. "Looks like he got lucky," Becky said, pointing to the IV line.

"No way. He did this mess." Barbara stroked her bruised arm. "They sent Maxwell himself to do the other arm. He's the top guy, you know. But I told him same as Coale, you got one shot at me. Maxwell *needs* only one shot!" Barbara laughed. "Which room you in?"

"With Mariela, come down and visit, OK?"

"I'm getting out tomorrow, my mom can take care of me at home, she's watched the nurses plenty. Dr. Maxwell likes to keep me in because I make him laugh."

"I kind of wish you were staying too," Becky said. "How long you in?"

"Long time, six weeks, maybe two months."

"Wow, what's wrong with you?"

"My leg, I'm having an operation."

"Well I'll probably be back. We go home and some bleeding starts, or I get a high temperature, and back we come."

By that night Becky felt as though she had been living in the hospital for years. When Theo called, Becky heard in her own voice the edge of politeness she used when talking to her grandparents with false jollity.

The surgery lasted eight hours; Becky was in the recovery room for three hours and was wheeled down to the ward, still sleeping, at nine o'clock at night. Loretta Romagnola had been hushed all day, silently offering Dick and Maggie Maitland fruit, coffee, sticky buns. Mariela kept the sound on her TV very low; whenever they passed the room, nurses made victory signs to the Maitlands.

It took three orderlies and two nurses to transfer Becky from the stretcher to the bed. Pillows raised her "new" leg about forty-five degrees; a maze of drain tubes and IV tubes was attached to the leg and both arms.

Maggie wished she could feel her daughter's pain. Becky was a stoic; for three days she had lain in a mummified silence, only groaning when the nurses irrigated her wound or rolled her onto her side in order to sponge her back or change the bedsheets. Becky sipped the juice and water her mother held out to her; she waved at her father and whispered hello to Theo and the boys on the phone, which her mother held to her ear.

Dr. Titelbaum had told Becky she could have pain pills whenever she needed them for the first forty-eight hours after surgery. She hadn't asked for any. The nurses were astounded at her self-control. Theresa told Mrs. Maitland wretched stories of other kids who had undergone the implant surgery and had thrashed around until they had to be restrained.

"Then there was the girl who whimpered for three days, begging for more drugs. Turns out she was hoping to get high on hospital sources. That Becky's a dream. You should be very proud of her. She's going to beat this thing; she's got the will," Theresa told Mrs. Maitland on the third day after surgery.

"Does it hurt much?" Mariela asked, when their mothers had gone downstairs for a break.

"No, it's better than chemo. The pain reminds me I don't have the tumor anymore. That's what I keep concentrating on."

"Leukemia's different. You can have a good blood count and two weeks later have malignant cells again. But I don't have pain except my legs hurt— bone pain."

"Titelbaum says my lungs are clear and he doesn't think the tumor cells escaped the leg."

"You mean the primary site," Mariela laughed. "I could pass for a doctor. I've been memorizing everything they say for three years. Ma doesn't know, but I go to the library at the Academy of Medicine and read about leukemia. She thinks I'm going to a movie with my friends. Instead I read hematology books."

"Hematology?" Becky asked.

"The study of blood. I can recognize the different types of healthy cells and malignant cells from color slides, and I figure I'll come across the name of a doctor we haven't gone to yet, one who has a way to cure it."

"Have you been other places?"

"Are you kidding! My mother calls the world, she

found a guy doing immunology work in Tokyo but he doesn't do kids." Mariela shrugged. "There was a research doctor in Peru but he won't touch kids either. He said he couldn't sleep nights if he experimented on a *child*. I heard Ma say to him, 'You'd sleep better if my child dies?' "

"Don't you think the doctors here are good?"

"I have a rare kind, nobody's any good," Mariela said curtly.

"But your mother says—"

"My mother thinks she'll frighten the leukemia away by yelling at it," Mariela laughed. "Actually I was in remission two years, that's the best they ever had with my kind, so they're all happy. I'm one of their successes."

"You aren't in remission now?" Becky asked gently. If she hadn't been rooted to the bed she'd have bolted from what she was hearing.

"There are plenty more drugs. Ma says when they run out of drugs here we'll go wherever they're experimenting with new ones. Our passports are ready. This time I'm in for a stupid infection. If my temp would stay down for twenty-four hours, they'd let me go home."

"Guess who's back?" Mrs. Romagnola sailed into the room. "The nurses gave me these flowers, Becky, your mother's bringing another bunch, are you ever the popular one."

Mariela touched one of the rose petals. "People sent me flowers when I was first diagnosed. Now I don't even tell people when I'm admitted."

"Keep those on your side," Becky said. "Oh they're from Rusty!"

"A boy, Becky?" Mrs. Romagnola asked. "Mariela got a bouquet from a boy who was here last winter. Bob. Was he a looker! If I hadn't been here, God only knows what would have happened."

"Ma wouldn't leave the room when he was here." Mariela rolled her eyes.

"Of course not. With you in a nightgown, in bed! No mother would have done differently."

"Look what Grandma Bacon sent, Becky." Maggie held up an arrangement of white carnations in the shape of a fluffly poodle standing on his hind legs. His tongue was three miniature rosebuds.

"What a joke," Becky chuckled. "Hey Mom, scratch my foot, it itches, oh Ma, get my foot." Becky pounded the mattress with her fist.

"Your toes are cold, Becky, you want a sock?"

"No, I'm fine, turn on the TV, Mom."

"Wouldn't you rather have me read to you?" Mrs. Maitland asked. "You haven't looked at your assignments."

"Mariela's getting me hooked on the soaps," Becky told her. "Let me goof off a few more days."

Mrs. Maitland said nothing. Mariela hadn't gone to school this year. "What's the good?" Mrs. Romagnola had asked in response to Mariela's questions. "What does she need with history and algebra? She was always an A student. What a joy she was."

Maggie vowed never to refer to Becky in the past tense. She became more determined that Becky would graduate with her class, and not become idle like Mariela, staring listlessly at TV all day. But for now, she would say nothing. Time enough to throw off the influence of the Romagnolas when they were discharged. Several times Maggie had caught herself nibbling one of Mrs. Romagnola's snacks when she wasn't even hungry. The boredom of a hospital room leads one to watching TV, turning the pages of magazines without reading them. As she fell asleep on her cot each night she could remember nothing of the day—other than holding the drinking glass for Becky or putting a sock on her healthy foot, or washing her face. The highlight of the day was talking to Theo and the boys—whom she had begun to think of as living on the outside.

She knew she wasn't being fair to resent her husband's going to work every day and stopping at the hospital for an hour each evening. He had to drive almost one hundred miles a day. His face looked more grizzled each evening. But during the day he was surrounded by familiar people, doing the work he always did while she sat in A26, listening to Loretta Romagnola rage against the hospital.

Sometimes Maggie prowled the halls looking for another mother to have coffee and a cigarette with. She was ashamed of herself for being unable to look at Becky's leg. When the nurses were irrigating the wound or bathing Becky or changing her bed, Maggie fled. When Dr. Titelbaum came in each morning, she focused on his trousers rather than watch him examine his work. He would exclaim proudly that Becky's wound was splendid; Becky was remarkable, able to joke with him and the nurses although she was not yet permitted to raise her head.

Becky was napping, as were Mariela and her mother. Maggie looked at her watch. Four o'clock. The boys would be playing outside. Theo had been surly on the phone when Maggie asked about school. Robin sounded like he was coming down with a cold. His colds always spread to his ears. She took her stack of magazines and her cigarettes and headed for the Parents' Lounge. At the end of the corridor she passed a room with a closed door. At Mercy the closed door is more powerful than a skull and cross-bones or a padlock.

Maggie could hear the hiss of oxygen and the implacable beep of the EKG machine. On impulse she pushed the door open a few inches to see the unfortunate child, so sick he was even separated from other sick children.

Through a forest of IV bottles she saw a tiny figure lying so still he seemed to have been ironed onto the sheets. A plastic oxygen mask cupped his nose and mouth. Wires led from his chest to the EKG machine, monitoring his heartbeats. The machine flashed and pulsed like a living creature.

The child glanced at Maggie without moving his head. She smiled but he didn't respond. There were no toys, no books, no stuffed animals here—the mark of a child too sick to play. She waved, closed the door, and glanced at the name card—Drew Murray. He was no bigger than Robin.

She settled herself in the Parents' Lounge, which was deserted except for an aide watching a soap opera. Maggie debated asking Loretta Romagnola about Drew. How could his mother leave him alone? Maggie tried to watch TV, but she saw that child concentrating on each breath. His stomach like a paper bag with a small animal panting inside it. She gathered up her magazines and walked back toward Becky's room. An aide bringing the juice cart around didn't stop at the room at the end of the hall. Maggie vowed not to open any more closed doors.

Walking past the children's drawings hung in the corridor, Maggie felt crushed by the weight of so much illness. Not all these children were as lucky as Becky. She had not thought she would again have occasion to think Becky was lucky. She smoothed the downy fluff growing back on her sleeping daughter's bald head and thanked God for all their blessings.

Almost as a coda to her prayers, a nurse came in holding a huge basket of red roses. She was followed by a hospital volunteer carrying an equally large bowl of spring flowers.

"What a luxury, flowers out of their season," Maggie said.

"Who're they from, must have cost an arm and a leg," Mrs. Romagnola said, yawning heavily.

"One thing we got plenty of here, Mrs. R.," Becky's voice sounded hollow from her flattened position. "Arms and legs."

"You can smell the roses way over here," Mariela said.

The volunteer set her basket down on Becky's nightstand. "There's hardly room for both these arrangements. Some fashion designer had a show today and sent over dozens of baskets. A lot of businesses do that. We try to encourage them. Silly to throw centerpieces away after a luncheon or fund-raising dance. Hotels just throw them out."

"Imagine going to a luncheon with such flowers," Mrs. Romagnola sighed.

Maggie inhaled the roses' fragrance. "What a lovely surprise. Tell you what, Loretta, after we get out of here, we'll go out for a special lunch, to celebrate." Maggie settled herself in her chair, the flowers giving her a sense of well-being.

Two weeks after the surgery, Dr. Titelbaum decreed that Becky's bed could be elevated to a semi-sitting position. Matthew came in each morning to work with Becky, showing her exercises to flex her ankle and foot within the limits of the brace. He taught her more demanding exercises with her left leg and her upper torso to prevent her muscles from atrophying.

"Take it slow, Becky. Titelbaum sees you twisting and turning like that, he'll put my butt in a sling."

Becky was delighted to have a physical workout. She had given herself a year from the day of the surgery to get into shape—she was going to stun Titelbaum and his flock by doing things with his metal bone that none of his other patients had done. She was going to ski, swim and run. Her first order of business when she was sprung from the hospital would be to walk without a noticeable limp. Even that would take time as she couldn't bear weight on the right leg for several months.

Concentrating on her exercises, she smiled at the wound, still concealed under layers of dressing. "You're going to heal smooth as glass," she said. "I don't hate you or the tumor anymore." She exercised ten minutes longer than Matthew had prescribed.

"Roll the left leg from the hip." Matthew was leaning over Becky, his hand on her left hip. He must know he's turning me on, Becky thought. Looking into his sunny face, Becky ached to spring from the bed and play a few sets of tennis with him.

"Don't I need exercise, Matthew?" Mariela asked. "I'm in bed all the time too." Last week Mariela had confided in Becky that she was crazy about Matt. "It was meant to be," Mariela had said, "I would never have known him if they hadn't put you in here. Isn't that a *sign*? He's a Leo. I'm a Gemini."

"Perfect combination," Becky said, pleased to be

talking about crushes and love instead of hospital gore.

"What kind of exercise did you have in mind?" He grinned.

"Anything you say," she answered coyly.

Becky was glad to hear life in Mariela's voice. Last night, half an hour before Mariela was to be discharged, Dr. Tang changed her mind and insisted Mariela begin a new ten-day protocol of antibiotics.

"I won't, I won't stay here, keep your fucking drugs," Mariela had screamed. She reached for a vase of flowers and hurled them across the room, soaking Becky's blanket.

Mrs. Romagnola rushed to clean up the mess, squatting over the broken glass. "If you say she's gotta stay, she'll stay," she said meekly to Dr. Tang.

"Ma! You promised! Ma! You promised!" Mariela sobbed.

"You can leave, Mariela," Dr. Tang said coldly. "We need the bed." She grabbed Mariela's wrist. "But if you leave today, don't come back."

A younger child would have jumped at the offer, Becky thought. Kathy or Barbara would go. But Mariela knows without the doctors she doesn't have a chance. Until Matthew had arrived this morning, Mariela had refused to speak to anyone. He's probably heard about it, Becky thought watching him tease Mariela. He's really kind; he cares about all of us. When Becky's therapy session was finished, Mariela came over to Becky's bed, her eyes shining.

"Did you hear him talking to me? Did you see when he put his hand on my shoulder? I told you he thinks I'm special!"

Theo threw her books on her bed. She had finished her chemistry final. She lay across Becky's bed. All the teachers had passed Becky with A's. She had no exams to take. She would not have to make up chem labs; in history and in English all she had to do was read and report on a few books. No surprise quizzes, no term papers.

"Come set the table, Theo. And bring down the laundry from the boys' room."

"Give me a break, Grandma. I just spent three hours on my chem final."

"Have you called Becky today?"

"No! I had two exams, for God's sake."

"Poor Theo! I'm sorry, dear." Her grandmother took an apple pie from the oven. "Would you like to ride up to the store on your bike and get some ice cream to go with the pie?"

"No I wouldn't like. Get the boys to do something. Everything falls on me," Theo said. "And I'm sick of it." She went upstairs and called Rusty.

"Let's get something going this weekend. We deserve some fun after exams all week."

"Will your folks let you? I mean with Becky in the hospital?"

"My name is Theo, damn it, and I have a right to some fun. People smile at me on the street, and say how's Becky, but no one says how are you, Theo.

It's horrible what's happened to Becky but it does have some advantages."

"Come on, Theo, she's losing her leg," Rusty squealed.

"Technically she's not. But if I say that I sound like a ghoul. How hardhearted can I be, right?"

"You can lay it on me, but I wouldn't advise saying it for the general public. It is a tragedy after all."

"Of course it is," Theo sighed. "Know what? I think I'm going to volunteer to stay with Becky during winter vacation. Maybe if I hang out at the hospital I won't be so pissy."

"Typical, Theo, one extreme to the other."

"You're not the first to notice that," Theo said.

She went downstairs and set the table. Then she went to her grandmother in the living room. "Sorry I was such a prune. How about I fix us some tea?"

"That would be nice. I made oatmeal cookies. They're in the red tin."

Theo ran for the cookies, her favorites. There were none in the tin, only a note on the counter from her father, saying he had taken the cookies and the Pepsi to the hospital. Not a word about my chem exam, Theo thought. She fixed the tea and rejoined her grandmother.

"Dad took the cookies, so we'll have to wait till the pie cools to get our sugar fix."

"He left already! I must have been napping. I wanted to give him some magazines for your mother."

"They do have magazines in New York, Gran."

"I wish they would let me visit Becky. I don't like being kept in the dark. Everyone so vague. I know she should be taking vitamin E. I read an article in *The Star* about vitamins in tumor cases. Shrinks them till they're the size of walnuts. I saw before and after pictures. They couldn't print it if it wasn't true."

"Becky's going to be fine. I'll slip her the vitamins. Doctors be damned." Theo kissed her grandmother. "I'm going to turn down that part in the play, it's silly. When Becky gets home I'll want to spend the time with her instead of rehearsing every afternoon."

"Of course you want to be with Becky. You girls have never been apart. Bring some vitamins for that other girl in Becky's room. Your father says she is not doing well at all."

Theo's heart clenched. What if someone died while she was visiting Becky?"

"Your poor father won't get anything to eat. The hospital cafeteria is closed by the time he gets there. He should take your mother out for a decent meal, they have to be alone, this coming and going business breaks up marriages," Grandma said ominously.

Hiding a smile Theo went to call her brothers for dinner.

"Can't you give me some idea what it's like?" Theo couldn't control her irritation. It was the first evening they were allowing her to visit Becky. She had been asking her father for at least twenty minutes how to act in front of the nurses and the other patients.

"It's a hospital, Theo. Don't make such a boiled dinner over it! Becky is in bed, her leg is wrapped in bandages. Most of the kids have no hair. Frankly I think the place has a *smell*, but your mother doesn't agree."

"What kind of smell?" Theo asked, thinking rotten eggs, rotten flesh. How can I act natural when Dad flies into a temper every time he comes home after visiting Becky?

"It doesn't matter. All you have to do is control yourself if some kid throws up in the hall. It happens." He leaned on the horn. "Did you see that guy pull out?"

Theo didn't answer. On the phone Becky was Becky. But she had not had an operation on her voice. I'll get a chance to do more acting in that hospital than I would have in the Senior Play, Theo thought.

"If you're uncomfortable, you can come home with me, Theo. We don't want to rush you into this."

"Of course I want to stay. It's only one night. Besides, Mom needs to get out of there. Robin thinks Mom is sick, you know. He doesn't say anything to you or Grandma but he asks me every day if Mom and Becky are getting better. He doesn't believe anything I tell him."

"Well your mother can straighten him out when she gets home." Dick Maitland leaned on the horn and cursed under his breath.

They were silent for the rest of the trip. Walking into the hospital Theo was surprised at how large it was. There were full-sized trees in the lobby. The floor was red and blue tiles. There were dozens of rattan couches and chairs covered in bright jungle-print fabric. Masses of red and yellow tulips spilled out of immense baskets.

"I'd never know it was a hospital," Theo told her father. "It looks like a resort."

"They've got a library for patients and a solarium for the kids on Becky's floor and a huge one overlooking the entire city for the adults. We can take a look if you'd like."

"Now that we're here I want to see Becky right away."

"You got it, ace. Elevators are this way."

As soon as they got off the elevator Theo knew they were in no resort. There *was* a smell, but what she noticed more was the silence. Her mother had said there were fifty kids on the ward. Becky talked about Mariela and Sally Beth and Richard and Kathy but Theo saw no evidence of people. The walls were decorated with kids' drawings. Theo glanced at the crayoned names and wondered how many had survived.

She was surprised when a couple of nurses passed them in the corridor. They were wearing pastel pants suits—they didn't look like Theo's idea of white-capped nurses. They were laughing loudly. Their high spirits seemed out of place. Theo remained solemn as they turned the corner to Becky's room.

"Becky!" Theo ran to her sister and stopped at the bed. "Becky! Can I kiss you? Are we allowed?"

"Of course." Becky held out her arms to Theo. She seemed to have grown since Becky had seen her. She sparkled in spite of the timid look she gave Becky. "Looking good, Theo! I have missed you, ask Mom!"

"Mom, I haven't seen you in three weeks either!" Theo hurled herself at her mother. At least she had the same body as when Theo had last hugged her. Becky was so hollow, so bony.

"Come here, Mariela, meet my sister."

Theo shivered at the sight of the girl sitting on the other bed. Becky didn't seem ruffled by her. There were great sores around Mariela's mouth, making it difficult to tell if she had ever been pretty. Her hairless skull gleamed. Her skin was the color of pie dough.

A boy wheeled himself into the room. His leg was stretched out at a right angle to his body. He had thick black hair. Theo thought he was probably fifteen or sixteen. She was impressed by the way he handled the chair, neatly avoiding the poles with bottles on them, and the shopping bags she had left in the middle of the room.

[167]

"You must be Theo. You really do look alike."

"That's Richard," Becky said. "He just happened to be passing by."

"Identical twins!" Richard looked at Theo closely. "And you don't have it?" he asked.

"You mean the tumor?" she said, wishing she had an answer.

"Shut up, Richard, you jerk!" Mariela turned to Theo. "He likes to get a rise out of people."

"Can you tell which is my good leg, Theo? They put a pin in it to stop it from growing. I was getting unbalanced," Richard said. He had beautiful dark eyes and the longest lashes Theo had ever seen on a boy. She pointed to the leg that was unbraced.

"Ha, that's the bad leg. Want to see my scar? For you I'll take off my jammies!"

Theo realized she was the only young person wearing clothes. Becky and Mariela and Richard were in hospital gowns and seemed perfectly comfortable with each other.

"No stripping while I'm here!" An immense woman spoke from a chair in the corner of the room. "I'm Mariela's mother."

Theo went over to her. "I've heard a lot about you, Mrs. Romagnola, nice to meet you." Theo hoped she didn't sound stupid. "Nice to meet you" in a cancer hospital!

Becky had become very fond of Mrs. Romagnola and was pleased that Theo was making a fuss over her. Becky wanted to tell Theo that around the doctors Mrs. R. was like a dog barking at cars. The moment one stopped she became docile, the bark a whimper.

When her parents left the room for the Parents' Lounge, Theo had an impulse to run after them.

"Becky, we have to tell Theo who everybody is! I am real glad your mom is letting you stay over. We'll have a good time," Mariela said. "If my Mom would go too."

"If your counts are good we may go home tomorrow. You wouldn't want me to go home and then you have to wait here if they say you can leave."

Theo couldn't imagine anyone sending Mariela home.

Becky wished she had had a moment alone with Theo to warn her about the deterioration in Mariela. This morning the doctors seemed angry at Mariela. Becky wanted to protect her friend. Don't blame her for not getting well. She's not pumping malignant cells into her body to spite you guys. Mariela hasn't eaten in five days. Why can't you help her instead of shaking your heads as you read her chart? She's not blind.

The talk of going home had turned flat. Mariela didn't answer her mother, didn't tell her she noticed the crowd of doctors outside the door grew larger each day.

Becky knew Theo needed time. "Why don't you find Mom and Dad? Go down this hall, turn right, and go to the end of the hall and there's a room

[169]

with clouds of smoke around it. They're in there, getting a nicotine fix. Go ahead, we'll wait for you," Becky smiled, hoping to relax Theo.

"I'll show you where it is." Richard turned his chair around. "I have to make my rounds anyway. Can't leave the fans without a glimpse of The King for too long."

"That's why we call him Richard the Crotch," Mariela said.

"Oh my God! What talk!" Mrs. Romagnola said from her corner. But Theo could see Mariela's mother was delighted that her daughter seemed to have pepped up since Theo's arrival.

Richard paused in front of a half-closed door. "This is Sally Beth's room. Blinds are closed. She's probably asleep. I'm going next door to see Rachel. Your folks are down there, see the room with the jazzy drapes?"

"They sure have a flashy decor around here."

Richard nodded. "It's to cheer us up." Richard squeezed her arm. "Tumor humor. See you later."

Theo opened the door to Sally Beth's room. Was Sally Beth talking in her sleep? She was lying flat on her bed, her eyes closed. The curtains were drawn; one dim light cast a soft glow on her serene face.

"I am taking the pain and attaching it to a parachute. A brightly colored balloon parachute. The pain is in the parachute and is flying up up up toward the clouds, into the great blueness. The pain is floating away. All the pain has left my body and is floating away. The pain is gone; the pain is gone."

Theo went back to Becky's room.

"I stopped in Sally Beth's room—" she began.

"You'd better stay out of rooms until you've earned your stripes," Becky warned. "Take it slow. Tell me, are you the captain of the tennis team?"

"I'm not playing tennis, Becky. Not without you."

"Nonsense," Becky sighed. "You are a much better tennis player than I am. You always were."

"You are just saying that to make me feel better." Theo sat on the edge of Becky's bed. "Did Dad tell you to build up my confidence?"

To Becky Theo did look pale, subdued. Becky had no sense of what Theo was thinking. She had always been a few steps away at school or the tennis court. Now she had to rely on Theo's versions of what was going on in her life.

"Are you playing volleyball? Swimming? Doing anything?"

"I tried out for the Senior Play."

"The Senior Play! What a joke!"

"I got the part," Theo stuck out her chin. "But I'm going to tell them to forget it. When you get home I want to be with you, not in some dumb play."

"Maybe it's time we did different things," Becky said softly. "If you really don't want to play on the tennis team. But don't give it up for me, Theo. You could be All-County, maybe All-State."

Theo shook her head. "It won't work, Becky."

"Did you talk to Sally Beth?" Becky asked, damned

if she would cajole Theo into playing tennis.

"She was talking in her sleep, lying in the dark *talking*."

Mariela laughed. "She wasn't sleeping, she was hypnotizing herself. To outrun pain. I do it too."

Theo looked green to Becky's eyes. "Come here, Twin-o, this is a big dose for you all at once." Becky squeezed Theo's hand. "We're all showing off a little."

Mrs. Romagnola hurried to Theo and embraced her. "They're monsters, trying to scare you."

"If we don't tell her, Ma, she might go into one of the bad rooms. Be careful about closed doors, Theo."

"Enough!" Mrs. Romagnola stumped around the room, gathering up candy wrappers and half-filled coffee cups. "Tell Theo about kids who are getting better, like you two. Tell her that Richard is here for his good leg. His surgery last year was completely successful. He's fine. Becky's fine and Mariela is going home as soon as she eats something and knocks out this infection."

Becky was ashamed of torturing Theo. "Remember when I dared you to walk through the haunted house in fifth grade? Well I just did it again."

Theo seized on Becky's apology eagerly. "It's OK. You sure had me spinning. Talk about trial by fire. Now can I join the club?"

Mariela kissed Theo's cheek. "You'll be my other sister." Theo hugged Mariela, amazed that she had not been repelled by Mariela's scabby lips.

"A few more hours in this place and I'll be ready to perform surgery," Theo sighed dramatically. She held up her hands like a surgeon preparing to scrub.

"Definitely you belong in the Senior Play," Becky said dryly.

Nine

The lunch trays have been cleared away; the doctors have made rounds and passed along the word to the flock of nurses following them about medication; they have ordered X rays, lab tests, spinal taps and bone-marrows. Patients needing tests or transfusions have overheard the orders. The kids scheduled for radiation are back upstairs. Nurses zigzag their way from room to room giving out the daily blood and chemo.

Barring emergencies there will be no more bad news or surprises today. If one listens hard, he can detect the sighs of relief after the doctors have signed their orders and left the floor.

"Looks good, Becky." Dr. Titelbaum gently pushed Becky's foot back toward the leg and examined her chart. "Flexing the ankle?"

"Every hour," she told him. "And I wiggle my toes, and— Watch this." Grasping the trapeze bar, she heaved her upper body six inches off the bed and held it for several minutes. "Matthew's a great coach!"

"I'm ordering more complicated exercises. Matthew will be up this afternoon. The danger of infection is past. You're halfway home, Becky."

Becky squealed. Mrs. Maitland looked radiant.

"She won't be able to bear weight on the leg, but if there are no complications, we should be able to throw her out of here in another three or four weeks." He chuckled. "Now don't make a liar out of me, Becky."

Becky bounced in the bed. "Told you I wasn't going to take your surgery lying down."

"My star implant," Dr. Titelbaum said proudly. As soon as he and his retinue of nurses and residents left the room, Mrs. Maitland reached for the telephone. "Wait till Daddy hears the news. And Theo!"

Becky frowned but Maggie did not pick up the hint. Mariela had been rushed back to the hospital last night after only three days at home. Becky had been lonely without a roommate but when Becky saw Mariela, pale and rigid with fear, she felt a crashing sense of defeat, as she knew Mariela did.

"A nosebleed, for twenty-four hours a nosebleed. Ice, compresses—nothing could stop it. Oh God, why!" Loretta Romagnola said, wringing her hands and resting her head on Maggie's shoulder.

During the night as shadowy figures of nurses came and went, Becky heard one of them say Dr. Tang feared internal hemorrhaging, and was ordering up enough blood for an army.

Since her arrival Mariela had not spoken. Occasionally she caught Becky's glance but she lay still, her eyes empty and unseeing. She had the sheets pulled up to her chin. Her mother had dragged her chair into a corner of the room and refused to sleep on her cot. All night she watched her daughter, her arms crossed over her enormous chest. They had left home in such a hurry, she had forgotten her coffeepot, a detail which both Becky and her mother noticed.

"It's good news, Becky," Mrs. Romagnola said from her corner. "Praise God. It is good to know He is still in the business of happy endings."

"I have a long way to go, crutches, the leg brace, and all that damn chemo," Becky said loudly, to drown out the happy laughter coming from her mother's telephone conversation.

Mariela said nothing. Becky bit down, her friend's rock-hard pain a weight on her own chest. "Please, Mariela, let's watch *Love's Brighter Day.*"

"You want to watch? You want me to turn it on?" Mrs. Romagnola demanded. Mariela didn't answer. She turned toward the wall, slipping her arm and its attendant tubes under the sheet, out of sight.

Becky wanted to call José. For about a week she

had watched the door, hoping José would make good his promise to visit her. She was afraid his silence might mean Titelbaum had been right.

"Think I'll go down to the Lounge, OK, darling?" Mrs. Maitland said. Her face was slightly flushed, as though someone had paid her a compliment. "Daddy was thrilled. He's going to drive in to celebrate with us."

Becky pulled her mother down close to the bed. "Stop carrying on, Mariela feels lousy. She doesn't need a victory celebration right in front of her eyes."

"But we must be happy, darling, it's such good news." She glanced over at the other side of the room. "I'll tone it down."

Mrs. Romagnola was staring at the TV screen with the sound off. This trip they hadn't brought Mariela's frilly nightgowns. There were no tins of homemade cookies, no jars of peach preserves, no pretzels, no hard candies, not even Mariela's slippers. A pair of gray hospital scuffs were under her bed, but Mariela had refused to get up. She insisted on a bedpan, refused to wash her face and stared straight ahead, limp and unresisting, while the doctors grouped around her bed.

"Hold up a second, I'll walk with you," Mrs. Romagnola said. "Mariela, OK if I go down the Lounge?"

Her daughter didn't answer.

"Don't worry," Becky said. "I'm not going anywhere. I'll ring—" Her voice trailed off. As soon as they had gone, Becky said, "It's almost time for Matthew. He asked twice yesterday how you were do-ing." Mariela didn't answer but Becky sensed she was listening. "He told me you were the best-looking girl on the ward. He even asked me for your phone number," Becky lied, desperate to make Mariela happy.

Her friend turned back toward the wall.

"What a business! Maggie, this time it's bad."

"There've been crises before, Loretta, you told me so yourself. Last year when she needed all those transfusions."

"If they could only get her back into remission."

"Can I get you some coffee or a roll?"

"I can't eat. Everything tastes like sawdust. You're a natural-born hoper."

"A what?"

"A hoper. Even when things are bad, you hope, and God makes it all right. Like Mary Tyler Moore on TV. Boy, I'd love to have your life for a week, like a vacation at an expensive resort."

"Is that how you see me?" Maggie said, her eyes wide with surprise. "It's been awful since Becky was diagnosed. You know—feeling that you've fallen down a well alone in the middle of the night."

"But you never wondered if this was the right hospital? If Titelbaum was the best surgeon? If Becky would make it?"

"I know this is the best hospital, and I guess we all wonder if our kids will make it, but Becky is strong, and if anyone can learn to live normally with that implant, it will be stubborn Becky."

"I was thinking of taking Mariela to a retreat in West Virginia."

"What sort of retreat?"

"Well, Francine Zeller, she was a Hodgkin's here last year, before you came, her mother joined Jews for Jesus, because she felt Jesus was a healer for all people. They went to this retreat run by a minister for a month and when they came back Francine had no malignant cells."

"Are you sure? Did they come back here to be tested?"

"No, they tested her down there. But they visited us at home. Mariela was in remission, and Frannie looked as good, maybe better."

"But she might have gone into remission anyway, Loretta. Hodgkin's has the best success rate these days."

"Her hair grew back real thick and she put on weight, she got color in her face, it was a miracle," Loretta said wistfully. "I don't want to live without Mariela, she's my whole life."

A nurse paused at the door. "Mrs. Romagnola, you want to talk to the social worker?"

She raised her tear-stained face. "Can she cure Mariela? Can she tell me why God is cruel?"

"Would you like me to call Father Murray?"

Loretta Romagnola dissolved into a fresh spate of tears. The nurse shrugged and walked on.

Becky reached for the telephone. She flipped

through her address book and dialed.

"Hey, José, is that you?" she said softly, not wanting to disturb Mariela.

"Who's this?"

"It's Becky, Becky Maitland."

"How are you?" The voice was barely audible.

"How you doin', José? I was hoping you'd visit."

"Don't have my strength back yet. Sister Rita Divine, she give me these herb powders, you drink them in hot tea, and you don't eat nothin' else. You understand? It be two weeks, and she say any day it's goin' to turn itself around. I be able to throw off the cancer because my organs be healthy again."

"You haven't eaten anything in two weeks?" Becky raised her voice.

"It's only till I purify my body, then I get lots of fresh fruit, but never meat again, the meat's what gave me the cancer. Knocked out my liver so it couldn't work. Then all the poisons stayed in my body. They had two prayer meetin's for me, one before New Year's and one last week." He broke off. Becky could hear him panting and coughing.

"Sister Rita does all kinds of cures. Once she brought a man back who had heart failure right during the witnessin'. And with this red clover blossom tea, I'm goin' to be saved. She soaked rags in some roots, she call it a poultice, and wrap it around my stump. There's only one bad thing—" José giggled and gasped for breath. "She made Mama give me these daily enema—"

"Oh, bleak," Becky said, wishing she didn't feel so sure that José's healer was a lunatic.

"But the worst part"—he coughed for several minutes—"it's made from catnip tea!"

"The enema!"

"You got it!"

"No, you got it," Becky was laughing too. "Listen, you really feel better, you got any energy?" Becky asked.

"Not yet, maybe when the liver get workin' right."

"I wish you'd talk to McNally or Titelbaum," Becky sighed.

"Shit, Becky, Titelbaum don't know any more than Sister Rita, he just know different stuff. She could have cured me without cuttin' the leg. It's against God, all this cuttin'." His voice was losing its strength. "Listen, I gotta go. Sister Rita and the Faithful be here for the prayer meetin' soon. You good to call me, Becky. I'm sorry they cut you too. But that's all Titelbaum know." José hung up.

Becky felt her heart pounding against her ribs. She was bolted to the damn bed. She couldn't run up to José's house and snatch him away from the Faithful. Automatically she thought of Theo. They had always worked in tandem. But Theo was at school, not bolted to a bed, but not within shouting distance of the hospital or José.

Even if Theo were at the hospital and Becky could convince her to go in search of José, Becky suspected Theo could do no better than say to him, "Becky told me to tell you." Theo couldn't understand the defeat Mariela felt at returning so quickly to the hospital. Theo, rosy with health, loomed above their beds when she visited. She looked out of place on the ward, like Reggie Jackson when he came to visit and gave all the kids autographed balls. Of course everyone had been stunned and dazzled by Reggie, but after he left Becky had heard grumblings, "What does he know about it anyway?" She knew kids grumbled about Theo and her hearty laughter.

Mariela was in no condition to talk about José. She's wondering if she'll ever leave again. Becky turned toward the wall. She couldn't bear to look at Mariela, wide awake, staring at the ceiling. She has to stay awake to protect herself. None of us, not even her mother, can guard Mariela. She must do it herself.

Becky wondered if she would ever go back to her old life. She was now closer to Mariela than to Theo. Mariela had told her one day when their mothers had gone downstairs for coffee that she did not mind dying. "If only I could have sex first. I want to know what it's like." She blushed faintly.

"Who with?" Becky asked.

"Not Richard the Crotch, maybe Danny—"

"Swell, Mariela. Know what Danny's in for? Testicle tumor, so much for Danny."

"There's only one man for me," Mariela said wistfully. "Matt. It would be perfect."

"Come here." Becky motioned to her. Mariela crossed the room, pushing her IV pole alongside her.

She sat on Becky's bed. "Did I hurt your leg?"

"Are you kidding? It's practically healed."

With Mariela sitting so close to her Becky could see all the veins in her hands. Perched on the bed in a hospital shift, her body had the flat planes of a seven-year-old.

"Just between us, sex is not so great the first time," Becky said. Mariela turned red. "You know!" she whispered.

"Well, I am two years older than you," Becky said dryly. "Anyway it's like any other sport, you need a lot of practice. I'm still a beginner myself."

"Minor league, the great Becky Maitland," Mariela giggled.

"You bet, only now I'm on waivers."

"You know Matt talks to me more than to any of the other girls. I think he might ask me out. It would probably happen. He's a Leo and they are very sexy."

Becky felt rage flaring inside her. After all the transfusions and spinal taps and blasts of chemo, Mariela deserved one dream. Holding on to bits and pieces of conventional morality was like trying to make donuts using only the holes. If any adult could admit Mariela had a right to try anything she wanted now, since there wasn't going to be any later, it would be Matt.

"What's going on in here, it's as dark as night, for God's sake, this hospital can't run without me."

[183]

"Sally Beth!" Becky's face brightened as the over-head light went on. "Mariela's asleep."

"When *Love's Brighter Day* is on? Mariela, are you asleep?"

"No. They brought me back last night because I had a twenty-four-hour nosebleed."

"What a bummer. I'm back for platelets. But I feel marvelous."

Becky was amazed. Sally Beth seemed to glow. Her face had lost its tightness; her eyes were open wide, as though she wanted to see everything in the world.

"Becky got good news. She can dangle her good leg," Mariela said, trying to look pleased. "I'm sorry I've been such a creep."

"Listen, I'm sorry my mother carried on so. I still have two years of chemo," Becky said.

"At least you have two years," Sally Beth said dryly. "I did a quick patrol of the private rooms at the end of the corridor."

Mariela sat up on one elbow. "We already know Drew's down there."

"No, he's not."

"You mean he's better?" Becky asked.

"Nope."

"Who's down there?" Mariela asked.

"Kathy," Sally Beth said flatly. "And they have all kinds of machines outside her room. The door is closed with the OXYGEN, NO SMOKING sign."

"We get good news with one hand and then this

happens." Mariela pulled up her sheet under her chin.

"There's more bad news," Becky told them, feeling as though all her strength had ebbed out through her incision. "I called José. His mother's got him hooked up to a healer. He hasn't had anything to eat in two weeks, just herb powders in tea. And he sounds like he's fallen for it. You should hear him wheezing and coughing—"

Sally Beth nodded. "That's 'cause it's in his lungs."

Mariela shrugged. "He might as well drink herb tea. Last summer his mother brought the healer here. She told us all that radiation cooks the flesh and chemo eats up the liver. Then one of the nurses overheard her and they threw her out of the hospital."

"How can people believe such nonsense, it gets me so mad." Becky thumped her pillow with her fist.

"José's not going to make it anyway, so why should he do the chemo trip? It's in his lungs, Becky." Sally Beth wheeled herself over to Becky's bed. "You know what that means."

"Titelbaum wanted to operate, he could have caught it."

"Titelbaum wants to operate because he's in a race with the cancer. After José refused to let him have McNally cut, you don't see Titelbaum rushing up to José's house to check on him. At least the healer pays him some attention. Once these doctors know you're on the way out, they lose interest," Sally Beth said.

"José's a failure to Titelbaum, not a person," she added viciously.

"That's not true," Becky insisted. "I get sick of you running this place down, why do you come here?"

"Don't get pissed," Sally Beth said meekly. "My mom doesn't have the bread for us to fly all around the world like Mariela's folks, searching for doctors. And she don't believe in any Sister Rita razzle. So it's Mercy for me. Besides Medicaid won't pay for healers here or in the Bahamas." Sally Beth wheeled to the window and pressed her forehead against the pane.

"I think this is the best place for us." Becky wiggled her toes. "I forgot the best part. José's got to have catnip enemas."

"Oh Jesus," Mariela howled. "I bet every cat in town is after his ass."

Sally Beth rubbed her cheek against the cool glass. "Look at those clouds. The sky is so blue. All the metal and plastic in this place makes me forget sometimes that we are creatures, God's creatures, like the wind and the sea and the trees."

Mariela looked at Sally Beth strangely. "What are you on?"

"Next time José calls, let me talk to him. We all have to help each other, hang together. At least here we are together. Maybe that's the best part of the hospital."

"When I started bleeding yesterday, I wished I was here. Ma got crazy, screaming orders and calling for the priest. And my father tried to stop the bleeding with one of his good shirts, and the dog was barking because everybody was yelling. It is better for me here too."

"There you are, Sally Beth. Go back to your room, hon, your blood's come up." Theresa checked the bottles on Mariela's pole. "You feeling OK, Mariela?"

" 'Bye, guys, I'll come down after the blood's run through."

"Hey, Theresa, do me a favor?" Becky asked. "Would you take this note to Drew for me?"

Mariela sat up straight.

"Drew?" Theresa straightened the blanket at the foot of Mariela's bed. "He's gone home."

"When, Theresa?" Becky said softly.

"Yesterday, I think. He wasn't on my side of the ward."

"Could you get me his address, I'll send the note to his house."

Theresa mumbled something and left the room.

"God, you are gutsy!" Mariela said, crossing the room to sit on Becky's bed.

Becky unfolded the paper. It was blank. "Just wanted to see what she'd say. They should tell us."

"They figure it's bad for morale."

Becky studied her friend.

"You're looking a whole lot better, Mariela."

"Guess I still have a chance, I mean, they haven't relocated me to the end of the hall."

"Damn right!" Becky glanced at the clock and began her exercises. "I bet those quacks really clean up."

"When I first got sick, my aunt found one who did the electrical cure. Some kind of current they shoot into the air from a little black box. My parents were all set to take me there, but the guy was sent to jail."

"What's wrong with doctors and hospitals, nobody in my family tried to give me catnip enemas, or shoot me full of *volts*."

"Maybe because your tumor was in one place, your leg, and once it's out, it's *out*. Clean. With leukemia, it's all over you." Mariela shivered.

"José had one of your *clean* tumors."

"Either they didn't get it in time, or it was not encapsulated, as the journals call it. His is metastasized all over his body, so it's the same as leukemia, I guess. Any cure is better than sitting around waiting for Johnny Miracle."

"Yeah," Becky sighed. "Looks like Johnny Miracle's going to be working overtime, poor José, all alone drinking herb tea. I wish they'd let him come back here, not for treatment but so he could be with us."

"I wish there was an island where we could go

and look after each other, we could lie in the sun and talk, I wouldn't mind chemo so much if we could watch the ocean and smell clean air."

"Somehow chemo doesn't seem right with fresh air and sunshine," Becky answered. "When I first was diagnosed, Sally Beth told me it was called bottled death. Each time they connected me to that tubing, I felt death dripping into my arm. I think that's what made me throw up."

"You, Becky! But you never say anything. Sally Beth is always trying to scare people talking about *croaking* and I stop talking altogether, but you seem so sunny, like it's all a piece of cake."

"I don't show it. But I wonder all the time if Titelbaum got it all. After all he was pretty cheery after José's surgery. Maybe it'll go to my lungs too."

"Not you. You look healthy. José always looked like hell."

"Really, Mariela?"

"I've seen so many kids. Remember how Drew would stare at the jars of paint in the Playroom, and never even dip his brush in. Just sit in his chair and wait, not asking anyone to take him back to his room, just *wait.* You have color, there're good juices flowing, you're going to make it."

"So are you. You look a million times better than when they brought you in."

"Last night I wasn't sure. I was really scared."

"I don't blame you. If I kept bleeding like that, I'd be terrified."

"I'm glad they put me with you." Mariela leaned over and kissed Becky. "It makes it easier."

"Hello, girls, one of you is Becky Maitland?" A doctor in a long white coat and dark skirt entered the room. "I am Adeline Brewer, I see by the paraphernalia you are Becky. So you are Mariela Romagnola. How are you today, Mariela?"

"Much better thanks. It was just a nosebleed."

"Of course. Would you excuse me? I want to talk to Becky for a few minutes." She smiled and pulled the curtain around Becky's bed.

"How are you getting along, Becky? I am sorry we haven't had a chance to talk but I am booked solid, you'd think I was Jane Fonda with my schedule."

"Are you a shrink?" Becky's tone surprised her. Maybe Sally Beth has taken possession of my mind.

"I am, but no reason to be uptight. We have a delicate situation and Dr. Tang and Dr. Titelbaum felt it would be productive for us to chat, that's all."

Becky had formed an instant dislike for the woman, who moved and talked deliberately, as though Becky were a spooked animal that needed calming. She's here to coax me back into my cage, Becky thought. "I don't have any problems." Becky wiggled her toes. "Unless you consider osteosarcoma a problem."

"Please don't be hostile, Becky. This chat is a bit irregular, I admit, but you are almost an adult, even though this is the pediatric service."

"Would you get to the point?" Becky asked. Maybe

I have become Sally Beth, she thought, and they are here to find out what happened to Becky Maitland.

"Here's the problem. Your roommate, Mariela, is unfortunately very ill."

"That's why she's in the hospital."

"You must be honest, examine your feelings, Becky. Would you prefer another roommate?"

Becky's hand started to tremble. "Is she going to be moved to the end of the hall?"

The doctor looked a bit unsettled. "What do you mean by that?"

Becky leaned toward the doctor. "Is she going down the hall, to the room where the kids die?" Becky spat out the words, hating the woman for her implacable face and perfectly combed hair.

"Perhaps a girl who has had osteo surgery, a girl who has shared your experience. It would be supportive for you both. You mustn't dwell on Mariela's problems."

"I am sticking with Mariela as long as I am here." Becky punched her braced leg. "If you send her to the end of the hall, I will get out of this bed and crawl down after her, tell that to the other doctors."

"You are overexcited, Becky. I am going to order a mild sedative."

"I don't need a sedative. You do. I'm not running scared. You are. Leave us alone. We would do better on an island, somewhere warm, where we could take care of each other."

"Becky, you are an intelligent girl. You must not

see the staff as adversaries, we want to help you."

"Is isolating kids at the end of the hall, with the door closed, separating them from everybody, your way of helping?"

Dr. Brewer stood up and smoothed her skirt. "We have many years' experience dealing with patients, Becky. We know what we are doing. If we seem cold, it is because we have to keep some distance. We've seen so many patients pass through this hospital, and other hospitals. It's the only way for us to keep control. It's not that we don't care. We care too much."

"Get out and leave us alone," Becky growled.

"We want to move Mariela because she seems to be depressed, we have no dark plan," Dr. Brewer said firmly.

"Depressed! Depressed! You don't know anything."

Becky turned toward the wall.

Ten

Theo stared out the car window at the refineries lining the Turnpike. "You think it *could* be from living near this mess?"

"What?" her father asked. He had been thinking how nice it would be to have his wife home, even for a night or two. She was so bland, so *pleasant*, when he visited, that he had no clear idea about what went on at the hospital. Maggie was afraid, even in the coffee shop, that a nurse might overhear her complaining and take revenge on Becky. Maggie was determined to ingratiate herself with the staff. It seemed to her husband as though they were house-guests trying not to inconvenience their hosts.

"Could Becky have gotten the big C from New Jersey?"

"I've told you not to talk that way. Nobody knows

how one gets a tumor," he added weakly.

Theo said casually, "Nothing I do pleases her, I feel like an outcast in that place."

"That's nonsense, Theo. Hand me some change for the toll."

"I call her after school to tell her what everybody's doing, and she says 'I can't talk now, tell me over the weekend.'"

"It distresses her to think about school."

"It's not my fault she's in there," Theo muttered. She slouched down against the seat. They wouldn't be satisfied until she gave up weekends with Freddy, dropped all her other friends and spent every free moment worrying about her valiant sister.

"Do you still worry that Becky might not make it?" Theo said, unwilling to change to a neutral subject.

"Not for a moment," her father answered rapidly. "We're going to beat this thing."

"What about Grandma Bacon? She calls every afternoon and hints that Becky isn't healing quickly enough. And Grandma Maitland carries on about that quack her friend went to and then tells me to remind you and Mom that she can get Laetrile."

"My mother is a jackass. Don't argue with her, it will only heat up her coals. And don't mention it to your mother. She's got enough on her mind."

"Every morning as soon as you leave to take the boys to school, she calls to see what kind of night Becky had." Theo opened her canvas bag. "She's into vitamin E cream. I'm supposed to rub it around

Becky's incision. *Plus* she said to Grandma Bacon it's a mistake to let me go to the hospital where I could pick up God knows what."

"So they're both idiots." He paused. "Mother may have gotten the impression from me that they don't encourage older people to visit. That unless it's *critical,* they shouldn't.'"

"Half the patients in the hospital are Grandma's age."

"She goes into her weepy act, we don't need any prima donnas at this point. And throw that ridiculous cream away. Next thing you know they'll be examining the entrails of a sacrificed goat."

"So that's why they never go to see Becky! You've thought of everything. I thought they were afraid. You know sometimes I'm worried about handling everything properly in front of the other patients—" Theo turned to face her father. "Sometimes I get panicked that Becky might not—"

"This kind of talk does no good."

"But you've seen those kids. So has Becky. Don't you think she's scared?"

"Theo, I won't hear any more of this." Mr. Maitland hit the brake and dug into his pocket for change at the tollbooth. "Becky knows that there are different kinds of—of—her illness. She had a tumor that was safely removed and she is going to be fine. The other kids have other *kinds.*"

"She criticizes everything I do, this whole thing is no picnic for me either."

"Did you remember the assignments for Becky?

If she's going to graduate in June she can't slack off."

"I have the trig and the history. She has to write an essay for English," Theo sighed. "It's not easy trying to *teach* her. I'm still in high school too."

They'll pass her and cluck over her because of the cancer. They'll make her valedictorian even if she doesn't do any trig assignments. A plus in surviving surgery for Becky Maitland. That's the name of the game.

"Did you hear me, Theo? Becky's ordeal won't be over when she leaves the hospital. Your mother says both Mariela and Sally Beth are in very *precarious* condition. Becky's grown attached to them.

"They have teachers at the hospital to help Becky. All you have to do is bring in the assignments. Surely that's not too much to ask," he said, his voice thick with sarcasm.

They resent me for being free of the cancer. Becky's so brave, the boys are so helpful to Grandma, everybody is a valentine except Theo, who has no rights, like she has no cancer. Theo, why can't you clean up your room, clean up your act. "Please don't sneer at me, Daddy," she said a few moments later.

"Your sister has been through a wretched time and you are whining because you're not getting enough attention. I am sorry for my tone of voice, but I am disappointed in you, Theo."

"I know you are," she wept. "And it's not fair."

"Would you rather stay home? I could stay with Becky so your mother can come home."

"That's another thing, I haven't seen Mom, I mean to talk to, in six weeks."

"God damn it, Theo," her father yelled, "what do you want us to do? You're worse than the boys."

"I'm worse than anybody, why don't you just say it." Theo smacked her fist into the dashboard.

"You are not going to goad me into a first-class fight, my girl. Clean up your act before we get to the hospital. With all the heartbreak you've witnessed in that place I don't see how you can carry on like this. I should think you of all people would understand how Becky feels."

"I know that, Daddy. But knowing that many kids are worse off than I am doesn't turn me into an angel. I'm still me. I don't know what it's like to have cancer and Becky hates me for not knowing." There it was, out in the open at last.

"I have no idea what you are talking about," he said coldly. "I do not want you talking like this to Becky. You are to give her support, is that clear?"

"Yes, sir."

Becky looked up from her chem notes as Theo and her father came through the door. "Hi, guys, Mom's down in the nicotine parlor. Look what Matthew brought me." She pointed to a button on her T-shirt that read *Cancer cures smoking*. "It's really for Mom but Matt didn't have the guts to give it to her."

"Now he's bringing you presents," Theo teased. Perfect Becky studying at the moment Daddy comes in.

"How's everybody at home?"

"We're all fine, but we'll be a lot better when we can all be together again." Her father leaned over and kissed her. "Titelbaum been in today?"

"Nope. I'm one of his old cases. After the first month he dumps us onto his resident. Unless he's showing visiting dignitaries around. Then he comes in, peels back the sheet, referring to me as the twenty-third case, and talks medical mumbo as though I'm not attached to the other end of his glorious work."

"I'll fetch your mother." Mr. Maitland nodded toward his daughters and left the room. The room made him uncomfortable. Mariela, poor child, was asleep with one bare leg on top of the sheets. Her skull bones were more prominent each time he visited. She reminded him of a high-fashion wooden mannequin to be clothed for a store window. Mrs. Romagnola had lost her effervescence; sunk into a chair in the shadows of the room her body looked like a sack of wooden blocks. She rarely spoke to her husband, who now came to the hospital each evening. He was a shy man who smiled nervously at the staff and his daughter.

"Hi, Theo." Mariela opened her eyes and sat up slowly. "What day is it? Saturday already?"

"No, vacation. It's only Wednesday. I'm here to relieve Mom. She is needed at home to tame the boys."

"My brother's been at my aunt's house so long, I don't think he even wants to come home."

Becky looked up surprised. "I didn't know you had a brother."

"He's too young to visit." Mariela shrugged. "Where have all the spectators gone?"

"Mine took yours out for lunch," Becky answered. "It's time for *Doctors and Nurses.*"

Theo laughed. "Don't you get enough hospital life in the hospital?"

"We prefer our doctoring on TV," Mariela told her. Becky was pleased to see Mariela so alert. Theo's presence was refreshing. Hospital routine caused what Becky thought of as defensive napping—nothing better to do.

Mariela glanced up at her IV pole. "Praise the Lord, they hung my daily blood while I was asleep. What service!"

"And do you know who gave blood for Mariela?" Becky leaned toward Theo. "Matt. Wouldn't I love to have his blood in my veins."

"I'll make you a deal. You can have my next transfusion if I can send *your* blood down to the lab as mine." Mariela pretended to be looking through a microscope. "What is this here?" she said in a good imitation of Dr. Tang's voice. "Today Mariela has all the good cells, her blood is beautiful, all those plump white cells, no malignant cells. Cured. Send her home."

"What station do we watch?" Theo asked quickly. "I'll turn it on."

"Is it time?" Sally Beth wheeled herself into the room and spun her chair in a circle. "Hi Theo, don't tell me you caught it?"

"No, I have a round-trip ticket."

"Turn it louder, I love TV docs. They're never puzzled, they never argue about drug protocols," Sally Beth said.

Becky knows they watch the soaps because the characters never hurt: Their pain is not real. The soaps are like cartoons in which a cat falling off Mt. Everest lands on his feet and merrily skips away. It's comforting to see the TV patients lying in bed wearing eyeliner and blusher. It makes Becky feel that Mariela would look healthy if she wore eyeliner. Becky can't explain the soap addiction to Theo in front of Mariela and Sally Beth. The one thing they are bound never to discuss is that Mariela sleeps more each day and hasn't left the room in a week. She doesn't eat anything, and her long painted fingernails resemble claws.

To break the silence, Becky asks Sally Beth about the gossip on the ward. "Did Ronnie go home? Has Richard sneaked into your room yet?" Becky turns to Theo. "Sally Beth has no roommate, she's too mean for them to put her with a little kid, and she scares the parents." Sally Beth nods proudly. "Richard, who thinks he's the heartbreaker of the hospital, keeps threatening to go to her room at night for a little kissy-kissy."

"I met him last time," Theo says.

"I wouldn't mind some kissy-kissy," Mariela says. "He's better than nobody."

"Wrong!" Sally Beth snorts. "He's a creep. You know, he can *walk*! I heard Titelbaum say he shouldn't sit in that dumb chair all day, but he'd rather go the sympathy route." Sally Beth is wearing a cotton bandana, its bright red color accenting her pallor. Her lips are blue because she has not received her daily transfusion. In spite of her languor, her voice vibrates like pebbles hitting a window.

"You ever notice it's *boys* who carry on." Mariela thumps her bed in disgust. "The tragedy kid, and he's wearing a brace and can walk without a cane in a couple more months. He may live for years."

"His hair is sure growing back gorgeous," Theo says and motions Mariela to move over so she can sit on her bed. "If he were harnessed to the bed like Becky, I might jump on him myself."

"He looked like a weasel when he was on chemo last year. Believe me, you wouldn't have looked twice at him," Sally Beth says.

"There's a lady volunteer in the clinic who thought we were brothers," Mariela giggles. "She used to say 'Want a lollipop, sonny?' every time I saw her, I must have told her a million times I'm a *girl*, he's a *boy*, and five minutes later she's back, 'Want a lollipop, sonny?' "

"Even without hair, no way you look like a sonny, Mariela," Theo hugs her and they settle back to watch the program.

Sally Beth turns up the volume. "Wonder if Lavinia will turn out to be very sick."

"Of course," Mariela says quickly. "The only other thing going is Susan having Martin's child and him thinking it's Bert's. Why do we watch such junk?" Mariela moves over a few inches to give Theo some of the pillow. "You comfortable?"

"We have to run a few more tests, it may be nothing," the TV doctor says to a green-eyed beauty with masses of chestnut hair.

"Where have I heard that before?" Sally Beth snorts.

"I've been so tired, maybe I need vitamins, I've been losing too much weight—"

"You know what it sounds like," Mariela is giggling and leans closer to the set.

"No, my dear, vitamins aren't the answer. Remember all the blood tests we've been running? The results have come in."

"She's got it, Mariela, you were right."

"My child, you're going to have to be brave, you must be strong, there are new forms of treatment." Dr. TV puts his arms around the girl.

"They played the same scene yesterday," Becky says.

Sally Beth snatches the scarf from her head and tosses it into the air. "She does have it! Tell her she's going to be bald," she snickers.

"We have miraculous new drugs, doctors are working all over the world." The girl sobs softly against the white-haired doctor's immaculate white-linen chest.

"Yeah and you throw up all the time, even pizza."

"What is it, Doctor? I am so afraid."

"You have—you have—" Organ music swells under his words.

There is laughter up and down the hall. Rachel appears at the door. "You have it on?" she screams. "Theo, wheel me in, I can't get my chair past Sally Beth's chair. My set's busted, lousy hospital."

Volume is turned up high.

"Carol, this is the worst part of my job, telling a beautiful girl like you, you have leukemia!"

The organ chords are drowned out by the shouts and cheers from Ava and Margaret next door and kids further down the corridor. It sounds as though someone hit a grand slam in the final inning of the World Series.

Mariela stretches out her left arm and gently shakes the tubes attached to her forearm. "Leukemia!!"

Becky sings, "You must be brave *tra-la,*" and falls back against her pillows.

Rachel smacks her stump, which is swathed in gauze and cushioned on a miniature waterbed attached to the wheelchair. "Jesus, why didn't somebody tell me you two have leukemia, I'm getting out of here."

"You sound like Uncle Butch. He hasn't come to our house since Ma told him last Christmas. She says he's afraid, him with those six kids. I might sneeze on one of them," Sally Beth says.

Rachel covers her nose. "Oh, I feel weak, I'm going to catch it, I'll have to get a note to excuse me from gym, I've got cancer."

"Only two of my friends know," Mariela says, breathing hard from laughing.

Rachel frowns at her leg. "It's not too easy to hide this thing. One guy came up to me in school and said, 'Were you in an accident?' I said very calm, 'No, I have cancer.' You should've seen his face."

Mariela's phone rings. Theo picks up the receiver and holds it to Mariela's ear, so the cord won't get tangled in her tubes. "Yeah, we were watching too, what about those wonderful new drugs!" Mariela talks for a few more minutes.

"That was Dana, she bet me they won't show a bald actress on TV."

"Right. Remember *Love Story?* No way Ali MacGraw was going to lie there bald. Who wants to go to a movie and see someone pasty and yucky?" Theo says, unmindful of Becky's warning signals. "She even had eyeliner on when she was dying."

Nobody says a word.

Sickened by her own stupidity Theo slides off Mariela's bed. Rachel squeezes her good leg, her lips pressed together. Becky cringes, knowing Theo is full of remorse but not knowing how to help her. Excusing her twin will make the situation worse.

Theo leaves the room, the girls' silence shattering her. She drifts down the hall looking for a place to be alone.

"Hey Theo, wait a minute." Sally Beth is wheeling her chair so fast the bottles are clinking on the pole connected to the back of the chair.

"I am such a jackass, my stupid mouth," Theo snaps.

"At least you realize what you did. Most people don't."

Theo smacks her forehead. "Becky'll kill me. I've been around here enough to catch on. What can I say to Mariela?"

"Nothing. That's the point."

Sally Beth wheels down the corridor. Theo leans against the wall. She thinks how careful the kids are with each other, how hard they try to spare each other pain. Unlike the piranhas at school. She recalls last weekend, she and Becky laughing with Frannie, whose parents took her to Europe during her first remission, and have promised her a car as soon as she's back in remission again. They groan with Mariela, whose grandparents take hundreds of pictures of her—Mariela eating, Mariela answering the door, Mariela watching TV, opening a present, polishing her nails, holding her fluffy dog on her lap.

Most of the children don't know how sick they are, Theo's parents have assured her. But now Theo knows otherwise. They know but what nobody talks about is that Mariela's been in relapse five months. The drugs aren't working anymore. She must be connected to those damn tubes all the time. Becky has told Theo one viral infection was following another. Mariela spikes fevers daily.

Theo pounds the wall, tears streaming down her face. God damn Ali MacGraw with her clean leukemia, clean and so pretty. Damn TV scriptwriters, Theo sobs, fools writing *leukemia* with an organ accompaniment, knowing nothing.

The following afternoon Theo was on her way to the coffee shop to get Becky a chocolate malted. A small girl approached her, taking the hesitant steps of an invalid. The child was pushing the inevitable IV pole alongside her.

"You're Becky's twin, right?" the child said.

"That's right, I'm Theo."

"Yeah, I heard about you. They won't let my brothers visit."

"The doctors aren't crazy about having me here, but since Becky's in for such a long time—"

"My brothers can't stand this place; my mother brought them to the clinic once. You should've seen them, almost passed out when they saw a blood bag hung." The child laughed. "They may be boys but they're cowards, both of them. They're scared of getting shots; they could never stand to be sick like I am."

"What's your name?" Theo asked.

"Barbara. Want to come to the Playroom with me? I'm making a candleholder for my mother and a bookend for my father."

"I'm going to the coffee shop. Want anything, ice cream?"

"I'm on medicine that makes you throw up. But thanks." Barbara paused. "Do you think Becky would like a mobile? I could make her one after I shellac the bookend."

"Honey, I think she'd love it."

"Becky's going to get better. She's going home to stay," Barbara said, leaving Theo speechless. As she made her way slowly down the hall, Barbara called back, "Keep your trap shut about the mobile. I want it to be a surprise."

When Theo walked off the elevator later that afternoon Sally Beth was parked in the corridor. "I've been waiting hours for you," she said to Theo.

"Becky and Mariela were napping so I went for a walk."

"Come down to my room. I have a plan, a dynamite plan that needs your help."

Theo wheeled Sally Beth down the corridor. "Aren't you going to tell me more than that?"

"It's Mariela."

"Mariela what? Come on, Sally Beth. You've never been exactly tongue-tied."

"She's a virgin, but not for long," Sally Beth laughed. "Get it?"

"She's fifteen."

"She's not going to be sixteen," Sally Beth said.

"You don't know that," Theo protested.

"She's told me and Becky she doesn't want to die a virgin. It's the only thing we can do for her, don't you see?"

"But no guy would agree to it, even if she could go home and we could introduce her to a guy, *yadayada lalalalala*."

"We're going to arrange it right here at Mercy."

"You'll excuse me if I don't take you seriously." Theo parked the wheelchair and sat on the empty bed in Sally Beth's room. "You had me going for a minute."

"It's all we can do to make Mariela happy."

"It sounds a bit kinky—leukemia, hospital, jail-bait." Theo raised the back of the bed. "Might be a good movie though. Mia Farrow could play a really scummy jailbait."

"With her it would be too sleazy. With Mariela it's going to be an act of love. Real love," Sally Beth said softly.

"Does she have a boyfriend? I only hear her talk about Matt," Theo said. Her heart was beating faster. Sally Beth couldn't mean Matt. Her face glowed, but Theo couldn't perceive her vision. "I want to understand, Sally Beth, give me a chance."

"Mariela's a sweetheart. She wants to know what

it's like to be in bed with a guy, is that so hard to understand?"

"Of course not, but how can we carry it off here?"

"After we get night meds, Mariela and I will switch rooms. Absolutely she has to convince them to take out her nasotube. She can't lose her cherry with a tube hanging out her nose."

"Becky won't break rules. When she was little she wouldn't scratch a scab because Mom said not to."

"She's graduated from scabs," Sally Beth said dryly. "It's hard for you to think like us, Theo. After chemo and surgery most things aren't important anymore. I used to hate my cousin because her folks are rich and she has her own car and lots of neat clothes. Sometimes I think I poisoned my own blood envying her."

Sally Beth's usual mask of defiance had disappeared. She slumped onto her bed and examined the IV board taped to her arm. "Ava's parents were on the verge of divorce. She got sick. Her parents stayed together. Nobody paid Richard any attention. Now they do."

"Becky disproves that bozo theory." Theo crossed the room and sat next to Sally Beth. "We can't wait till she comes home. Especially me. Then we'll be twins again."

"She'll never be the same, Theo. None of us are."

"But you believe you'll get well, don't you?"

"If I didn't would I be hooked up to all this stuff? A few weeks ago I was sitting on the screen porch.

It was one of those January thaw days. The sun came out and shone on the couch where I was. It smelled like spring. Suddenly I knew I was part of the sun and the frozen ground. The sun went behind a cloud but I could still feel its warmth. Since then I haven't had any bone pain. But I can't go back to being your standard high-school kid. Neither can Becky." She squeezed Theo's hand.

Theo stared at their fingers. "I never told anyone this, but ever since Becky got sick, I've been *counting* everything. Like there are thirteen stairs between floors at school. So I ask God to let Becky live thirteen more years. Last week I counted the branches on the forsythia bush outside our living room, and prayed that God would give Becky more time than those thousands of buds. Then I thought I was asking Him too much, so I changed it to more months than the twenty-nine or thirty biggest branches."

"My aunt gave me a five-year diary last Christmas. I threw it across the room. It broke a mirror. Don't think I didn't get the creeps from that." Sally Beth released Theo's hand. "So you see why it's important that we do what we can for Mariela."

"What about Mrs. Romagnola and my mother?" Theo slicked her hair behind her ears. "Setting up a love tryst beats counting cornflakes in a breakfast bowl."

"I knew you'd do it. Mrs. R. won't be easy. She sticks to Mariela like glue. Unless we tell Mrs. R.

there's going to be a Bake-off in the Playroom and she's elected to judge the cakes. She'll go to the coffee shop for a warmup session."

Theo shook with laughter. An urgent glance from Sally Beth sobered her quickly. "We got the girl and the room. Who's the guy!"

"Matt of course."

"He'd lose his job."

"No one will know. He'll understand why it's so important. He comes in on weekends to visit the kids whose parents can't come. He brings us candy and silly stuffed animals."

"Well I can't ask him, I don't even know him." What if Mariela checks out while they are—? Theo banished the thought.

"Becky will ask him even if she pees in her bed while she's doing it," Sally Beth said. "She loves Mariela."

"And what about Mariela? Talking about it is one thing but what if she chickens out? Maybe she's too sick now?" Theo said uneasily.

"So, they can hug each other and fall asleep—but together," Sally Beth said cheerfully. "We'd better get cracking. It's going to take a little foreplay—no pun intended—before we can maneuver the doctors into removing our tubes. She's got to be *mobile*."

Theo looked at her fondly. "Let's go rope Becky in. After all, in the old days kids our age had kids of their own." With a great flourish Theo wheeled Sally Beth out of the room.

Eleven

Mickey Maitland paused at the door to his sisters' bedroom. With Theo in New York the room was unnaturally neat and quiet. He couldn't recall when both twins had lived there. He sat on Becky's bed. Had it been two months since he had seen her? Some days he couldn't remember her face unless he sat on the stairs and looked at the framed family pictures.

He dreaded Becky's leg. Would it be skinny like a piece of clay rolled out long between his palms? Would it quiver like spaghetti dangling from a fork?

Ever since Becky had gone into the hospital, Mickey had kept his eye out for people with a bad leg. But in the shopping center and around school everybody was normal. Except for Carlos, who had no legs and sold comic books from his wheelchair outside McDonald's.

Mother had promised Mickey that Becky's doctor was the best in the world. When Becky's leg healed it would look normal except for a scar. But hadn't Becky been away too long to come home normal? He had heard his mother sobbing late at night; he had listened to his grandmother telling her friends how brave Becky was. If her leg was going to be normal, there would be no reason for Mom to be in New York with Becky for two months. No need for bravery. All the evidence pointed Mickey toward one conclusion—when they finally pulled the bandages off, the leg would be red and wrinkled, worse than his arm had been after the cast came off. Since Mickey hadn't needed an operation or two months in the hospital in New York City, his arm had healed. Dad told him Becky had not broken her leg. Mickey had seen that for himself. She didn't have a cast like his, plus she hadn't had an accident. No getting around it. The leg would be hideous and he would be expected to pretend it was normal.

He knew when this would be. Next summer—the time for bathing suits and shorts, when the leg couldn't be hidden inside jeans.

Tears rolled down his cheeks when he thought that now people wouldn't confuse the twins. He wondered if Theo knew they weren't twins anymore. But he was afraid to ask her. Whenever he asked questions, people flew at him, never giving him a chance to explain that he still loved Becky. Why wouldn't any of them tell him the truth!

"Mickey, want to play miniature golf?"

Mickey jumped off the bed and ran down the stairs. "Do you have time, Mom? What about the hospital?"

"Theo just called. Since the doctor's away at a medical conference she wants to stay with Becky an extra day and I want another day home with you guys." She opened her arms and he ran to hug her.

"You know Robin's lousy. When Grandma took us Robin racked up the worst score they ever had in that place—ten shots and he still couldn't get the ball through the covered wagon."

"It's his first year playing. You were no star yourself, old boy."

"Then he throws his club on the ground and acts like a brat."

"Would you rather not go?"

"I hate it when people who aren't normal get treated special, don't you?"

Maggie sighed. "We could go to McDonald's for lunch." She was too tired to ferret around in her son's head to find out how deep this "normal" business went. Before Becky was diagnosed Maggie had prided herself that she left no loose threads in the fabric of her children. Now she could only hope the thread didn't unravel into a major rip.

"I hate McDonald's, Mom."

"Since when?"

"I hate that cripple selling comics."

"He's doing the best he can."

Mickey glared at his mother. She used to be good at deciphering his codes. "I'll look for Robin. We'll meet you in the car," he told her. Then he smiled politely, as though she were a neighbor offering the boys a ride to the golf course.

Becky was reading about the Wars of the Roses. Mariela was down at X-ray. For the first time in six weeks Becky was alone. She relished the silence. With her mother at home, Becky felt less like a patient. It was a help having her mother as a private functionary, handler of bedpans, fetcher of magazines and malteds. Rachel had stories of waiting forty-five minutes for a nurse to answer the call bell, by which time Rachel had already soiled the bed. Sally Beth's hand was swollen for a week after her IV had infiltrated while the nurses were in one of their meetings. Mrs. Maitland had become great at buzzing the nurses' station, glaring through the glass until a nurse followed her back to Becky or Rachel or Sally Beth, for whom Mrs. Maitland now served as surrogate mother.

Becky had stopped missing her brothers. She no longer looked at the clock and wondered what would be happening at school or at home.

"Where is everybody?" Sally Beth appeared in the doorway. For a moment Becky didn't recognize her. "What happened to your wheels?"

Theo wheeled herself alongside Sally Beth in the doorway. Becky studied Theo. Her sister was clumsy propelling the wheelchair. She was flushed and giggly, as though she were at a pajama party. Pushing her IV pole, Sally Beth walked to Becky's bed. "Still very wobbly, but I need more mobility than the chair allows."

"Mobility," Becky sighed. "When I get out of this harness, I'm going to stand for a week, day and night, leaning against a wall if I get tired, but standing on two legs!" She spoke fervently, one hand gripping each thigh.

"Mariela's not responding to the drugs," Sally Beth interrupted. Theo got out of the wheelchair.

"She has been sleeping more and she doesn't seem interested in anything, not even TV," Becky conceded.

"Remember what she said about wanting to have sex?"

"That tore me apart too."

"We can fulfill her wish."

"Us!"

"Theo and I worked out the details yesterday. We are ready with a plan."

"Don't let Theo use your wheelchair. The nurses might get mad. We have to keep the peace."

"It's got to be Matt."

"You've lost me," Becky said. "What Matt?"

"Mariela's *lover*," Theo said. She felt wonderful, sharing with Becky again.

"Are you nuts?"

"That's why I'm walking," Sally Beth told her.

"Mariela will have to ditch her chair too. So we can switch rooms after night meds."

"You are nuts."

"You have to convince Matt that we need him."

Becky socked her head against the pillows a few times.

"This is all a joke, right?"

"It's all we can do for Mariela. You know how she carries on about him," Theo burst out, hoping Becky wouldn't resent her taking part in the plan. Becky was touched by Theo's face, pinched with intense concern.

"We are all in a lifeboat," Becky said softly. "I hope I can convince him."

"We're back, stop talking about us," Mrs. Romagnola sang out as she pushed Mariela's chair into the room. Looking guilty, Theo fled. Becky tried to get Mariela's attention, but she was glum, listless.

"You want to sit up awhile, Mariela?"

"Leave me alone, Ma!"

Mrs. Romagnola scuttled back to her chair in the corner.

"Mariela, what about coming out on the sundeck," Sally Beth said, retying her head scarf more tightly.

Mariela looked up. "It's not even March, it snowed last week!"

"Got your attention!" Sally Beth smiled triumphantly. "We will see you later. Becky has to work with Matt this afternoon and you have to work with me." Sally Beth pushed Mariela's chair with one hand and her IV pole with the other. Their progress was very slow until Mariela began to guide the chair by rolling the wheels forward.

Becky could hardly call Matt with Mrs. Romagnola like a large brooding bird in the corner. Sally Beth's plan couldn't possibly work. Certainly Matt would refuse. Then there were the mothers to get rid of, not to mention the reaction of Mariela to Sally Beth's scheme. Becky suspected it couldn't work physically. Mariela didn't have the will to brush her teeth. Anything more strenuous seemed out of the question.

Becky closed her book and feigned sleep. Mrs. Romagnola was sighing every few seconds, one of her preludes to a tirade about the staff.

"An hour they keep us waiting in X-ray. Mariela shouldn't be waiting in that hallway. She'll catch a draft and they'll make us stay another week. You know she's not really angry with me. It's the nurses she hates. She takes it out on me because she's afraid they'll stick her extra if she complains. She and I are much closer than mothers and daughters."

Becky murmured from her bed, "She tells me all the time how much she needs you here."

"Ma, go home for the night. I'm fine and Dad and Tony miss you a lot."

Becky couldn't believe this perky creature was Mariela.

"Mariela, where's your chair? You're walking," her

mother ended in a sob. "Thank the Blessed Mother. I knew it was a virus, didn't I tell you, it wasn't the leukemia, just a virus, like anyone gets."

Mariela's face was flushed. "And tell the nurse they can take out this stupid nasotube because I am going to eat. I don't feel nauseous anymore."

Her mother wept, "My baby, I knew you would get better. Mother of God, a miracle!"

"Ma, it's not a miracle." Mariela walked over to her mother. "Don't get your hopes up, just go home for the night. Please!"

"With you getting your strength back? You need me more now than ever." Her mother stopped crying and smiled broadly. "I'm not budging an inch!"

Mariela crossed to Becky's side of the room and lifted her left arm, from which the coils of tubing hung. "Ma, if you don't leave, I'm going to yank out these tubes."

"Mariela." Her mother hunched her shoulders.

"Ma. I'm sorry. I didn't mean it." Mariela's eyes implored Becky to help her.

"After all, Theo will be here. If Mariela needs a nurse, Theo will track one down. *My* mother left. She said when she comes back, she'll be refreshed," Becky spun the words carefully. As she might cajole Robin.

"Right Ma, you'll be refreshed." Mariela went over and kissed her mother. "Please, Ma, I'm begging you." Mariela's voice rose.

"I'll call your father," Mrs. Romagnola said. "If

he says OK, I'll go. But I will be back tomorrow morning before rounds." Mrs. Romagnola scrutinized her daughter, trying to make sense of this magical transformation.

Becky plunged on. "You know what José told me my first day of high-dose? This will give you a laugh, Mariela. He talked for about two hours to distract me. All the while he was getting Cytoxan! I had just told Mom to drop dead—oh I'm swell when I'm getting chemo. José said, 'Hey Becky, listen what I'm telling you. You know what Titelbaum suggested. He said, We can't make your leg better, José, but I'll touch up your X rays so you won't be embarrassed at grand rounds when they all examining your *case*!'"

"Just like those damn doctors," Mrs. Romagnola fumed. "That poor boy, not once did I see his mother here. Women like her don't deserve children."

"Ma, it was a joke, Titelbaum didn't really say that."

"How do you know?" her mother answered darkly. "Now get in bed before you start to bleed. Remember last time."

"Guess I'll call Matthew," Becky said in hopes of breaking up the fury on Mariela's face. "Think I should, Mariela?"

Mariela held her face in her hands. "I guess so," she said softly. "If Ma goes home."

"What does my leaving have to do with Becky's therapy?" her mother said. "Are you girls cooking up something? Well, what can happen in a hospital?" She laughed. "OK, I'll call Daddy. He can pick me up when he gets off work."

"Then I'll call Matt," Becky said, carried away with the enormity of what they were about to do.

"Hello, Selma, it's Becky Maitland. Would you ask Matt to come to my room?"

"Ma, get me a malted! Tell the nurse we need Tang to take out this nasotube before supper."

"A malted she wants," Mrs. Romagnola shouted into the telephone. "Praise God, it's a miracle. She's eating!"

"Ma, stop making a big deal."

Mariela looked down at the hospital shift. "Becky," she called. "Look at this *thing*! I have nothing to wear!"

"I only have T-shirts," Becky said. "Maybe Sally Beth—"

"What do you need to wear," Mrs. Romagnola burst out laughing. "You're going maybe to a dance?"

"Ma, look at this thing. It's hideous!"

Becky reached for her telephone. "I'll call Sally Beth."

"She's with Kathy, down at the other end," Mariela said.

Mariela went into the bathroom and closed the door. She took off her shift and looked in the mirror. Her forearms were black and blue from the IV needles. She hadn't had time to heal before another vein was punctured. She looked proudly at her con-cave belly. She had finally lost what Ma called her love fat. Her eyes went back to her chest. She was almost without breasts. Her nipples were dark brown and shriveled like raisins. When she thought about Matt she felt light-headed. She sat on the edge of the tub and ran her hand over her breasts. She shiv-ered from the cold plastic of the tubes. At least they would be gone by the time she went to Sally Beth's room tonight. She'd look like an ordinary girl. She rubbed her palm over her head. It was stubbly. Short hairs had been growing back since Tang had stopped chemo three weeks ago. Mariela sighed. Her head felt like her father's cheeks when he didn't shave. How could she go through with it? She wasn't a girl. She was half a person, filled with other people's blood, pumped up on medication and megadoses of vitamins that bought her skin a little color, herself a little time. Matt would be revolted. She loved him too much to ask him to do something hideous. She glanced at her pouchy little breasts and felt all the energy the plan had infused in her give way to dis-gust with her repulsive body.

"Mariela, you OK?"

Theo was banging on the door. "I got you a pres-ent. Come see it."

"In a minute, Theo. I'm on the john."

Mrs. Romagnola looked up from her chair, which she had pulled into the center of the room. "See, no bedpans, she is better. God's will be done."

Becky wished Mrs. Romagnola didn't look so radiant. In a few days she'd be hunched over, holding her head in her hands, rocking herself, the way she did when Mariela was in trouble.

When Mariela came out of the bathroom, Becky was surprised. She had tied a scarf around her head, the sparkly Mariela Becky had first known. Maybe it was a miracle!

"What did you get me?" Mariela sat on her bed and opened the fancy box Theo handed her. It was a short white nightgown as fluffy as meringue. "Try it on," Theo said.

"Oh Jesus," her mother gasped. "What a thing! You look like a bride."

"Oh Ma!" Mariela winced. "Don't say things like that."

"You want to get rid of me. I'll see you tomorrow. Remember, if you need me, call. Theo, here's the number. Keep it with you. I can be here in forty-five minutes. You call me, Mariela, before you go to sleep." She kissed Mariela, Theo and Becky, then she went back and kissed Mariela again.

"Ma, if you don't leave—"

"OK, I'm going. Hello, Matthew! Look how they treat me, trying to get rid of me because Mariela is feeling better. She's drinking a malted, she used the toilet."

"Ma! Shut up!" Mariela turned scarlet and buried her head in her pillow. "Just go, please!"

"As long as there's no emergency, sugar, I'll be

back later." Matt looked uncomfortable. "There's a sale on emergencies today."

He can't refuse, Becky assured herself. He had been at the hospital long enough to understand. Even Theo seemed to sense the rules for this special game of survival. A few months ago Becky might have been shocked. But arranging sex for Mariela seemed a positive step, higher up on the ladder of survival tricks than those mammoth stuffed animals Mariela's relatives sent her.

Becky had been so careful not to tell Theo she had slept with Jay. That was a million years ago, Theo a different sister. They had vowed when they were twelve they would lose their virginity on the same night. They had gotten their first period four days apart. Theo had said she hated those four days, waiting for Becky to catch up.

Becky had heard Mariela scream "fuck" at her mother and at a horde of doctors, had smelled her friend's vomit and shit. How could she and Mariela re-enter the land of "please" and "thank you?" Giggle when somebody farted in class?

She did not think about Mariela's "chances." When Theo had first come to the hospital Becky could have choked her. Eyes dilated with excitement, Theo had whispered, "What's she got, is she going to make it?"

Becky had tried to explain. "We don't think about who survives and who doesn't. Each day is a separate life. Will the white count be higher? Will there be pain or awful tests? Will the doctors be pleased? The cue for the mothers to twitter in their chairs, repeating with joy, 'He was *pleased*, he was *encouraged*!' "

Theo's confusion was unmistakable. So Becky had not told Theo that life in the hospital is the opposite of what it appears to outsiders. Mariela screams at her mother but she needs Mrs. R. more than she needs the drugs. Becky knew Theo couldn't bear to touch her leg. So Becky did not tell her, "I don't hate my leg the way I did in the beginning. The metal bone and plastic tendons are part of me, they are not the enemy. The tumor was not the enemy." Theo would be stunned if Becky told her, "My fear of the tumor was the enemy."

When Titelbaum praised Becky, saying "Your lungs are clear, your counts are good, we're very pleased," she felt like an impostor. After all, she had no control over her blood cells or her lungs. Since she could see the bandaged and braced leg she felt more kin to the excised femur than she did to her well-functioning lungs.

When Kathy's mother had told Mrs. Maitland that they had found a new tumor in Kathy's stomach, Becky tried to imagine how that must feel to Kathy. Was it like a bellyache? The flu? Was a brain tumor a humongous headache? Life on the ward, where parts of the body were gossiped about like wicked or conniving people, taught Becky that she had no idea what went on under her skin. Her body, close as a heartbeat, was as unfathomable as another galaxy.

Theo was polishing Mariela's nails when Sally Beth burst into the room. She leaned against the wall, her head flopped forward on her chest.

"What is it? What happened?" Mariela ran to her, waving her wet nails high above Sally Beth's head. Theo helped her into the yellow armchair and Becky adjusted her bed to the upright position.

"I went to see Kathy. I saw her mother go into the social worker's office so I thought I'd go talk to Kathy, since she's all alone down there."

Theo handed Sally Beth a box of Kleenex. Sally Beth squeezed the box, then hurled it to the floor. "That's it. *Kleenex boxes*! I'm standing at the door. Kathy pretends she doesn't see me. Finally I go into the room. She has put her Mickey Mouse doll in one Kleenex box, her Miss Piggy in another. Then she holds up two hugging brown bears. 'Should I bury them in one box or in two?' she asks, her voice so hoarse I can barely understand her. Then she tells me to hurry up, she has to finish burying them before her mother comes back. I say 'Put them in one box,' so she jams them into a box. Then she asks me to bury the boxes under her bed because they're all dead now.

" 'When you die, they bury your body,' she says to me, 'the cemetery is under my bed.' So I line up the Kleenex coffins under the bed and then she asks to see them to make sure I did it right. She

[226]

holds out her arms to me and I lift her off the bed. She doesn't weigh anything. She's like a butterfly. I lower her to the floor. She sees the boxes and kisses me. I put her back in bed and she looks at its empty corners, where her animals used to be. Then she starts crying, so hard no sound comes out.

" 'Nothing is left,' she whispers."

The girls say nothing. Becky turns her head to the wall. A nurse comes by and shuts the door to the room. Theo hears another nurse going down the hall, closing all the doors.

"Why are they closing the doors? Naptime?" Theo asks, to lighten the mood Sally Beth's story has cast over them.

Sally Beth beats her fists into the air. "It's Kathy, I know it's Kathy. My God, I was just talking to her!"

Theo hurries to Becky. "Does she mean—"

"They close all the doors when somebody croaks," Becky snaps. "It's not Kathy. It can't be, not so fast." She speaks across Theo to Sally Beth.

Mariela shakes her head slowly. "It's God telling us what we planned for tonight is wrong. It's against God. I knew it was but I hoped—"

"Nonsense," Sally Beth says, fighting off her own hysteria. "Whatever has happened has nothing to do with tonight."

"Everything here is against God," Theo says, finally beaten by Mercy.

"Where the hell is Matt, probably screwing a nurse," Becky wails. "Can't depend on any of them."

"It *is* Kathy, after all she's been down the end

for two weeks, they usually put kids down there for the last couple of days." Sally Beth looks at Becky. "There's so much I should have said to her. I've saved all the pictures she drew for me. I never told her."

"Stop. It can't be Kathy." Mariela smoothes the layers of ruffles on her nightgown.

The door opened and Dr. Reynolds, one of the new residents, came in. "Hello, girls. I'm here to take out your tubes, Mariela."

"Forget the tubes!"

"And what a lovely gown, you are a lucky girl!" The girls saw that they made him nervous.

"Get out! I'm keeping my tubes and I'm changing back to my hospital gown." Mariela shuffled into the bathroom.

Sally Beth held her hand up to the resident. "Don't go. Those tubes are coming out." Sally Beth stood up and walked to the door of the bathroom, wiping the tears from her face. Composed she turned back to Dr. Reynolds. "By the way, was it Kathy?"

"I don't know what you mean," he replied blandly.

"We *know*," Becky said impatiently. "When they close the doors, it means one of the kids has died, *we know*."

Theo heard the bitterness in Becky's voice, saw the hardness in her eyes. There was a face inside Becky's face that altered her expression. Her smile was no longer Theo's.

"I can't give you privileged info, Becky, ask your

doctor," Dr. Reynolds shrugged. "I'll be back to disconnect Mariela."

"He fled," Becky said and threw the pillow supporting her arm to the floor. "I've had it with these IV's, no more chemo."

Theo ran to Becky and held her arm gently. "Please, Becky, you're almost free. You don't have a tumor anymore. You're not sick anymore."

Becky calmed down. "What the hell is Sally Beth doing to Mariela in there?" She shook her head. "I'd rather cross a doctor than Sally Beth." Theo propped the pillow under Becky's arm.

Theo was drawn to the room at the end of the hall. She inched down the corridor, trying to stay out of sight of the nurses. The end of the corridor was dark, silent. She got to the door of the room, surprised that it was open a crack.

Her heart hammering, she peeked inside. Kathy was lying in bed, her arms outside the covers. There was no one else in the room. Theo had opened the door a little farther when the child's head turned and she snapped, "Get out of here!"

Theo slammed the door and fell back against the wall, her knees shaking violently. The child so near death fascinated Theo. She opened the door again and stuck her head in. "Can I come in for a minute? I am Theo, you remember? Becky's twin?" As she talked Theo approached the bed. Kathy's head was covered with black fringe, pieces of hair poking up at odd angles. Her bushy eyebrows arched over her eyes in a dark furry line. Her skin was transparent, bluish veins were visible all over the child's arms. She was fragile as a teacup. Only her husky voice remained vital.

"You know what happens when you die?"

Theo shivered. She shook her head.

"God comes and gets you in the car."

"Where does he come?" Theo asked softly.

"Downstairs outside the lobby," Kathy growled.

"Where does he take you?"

"He drives you to heaven. You stay there till you get better."

"Then what happens?"

"Then God drives you back."

Kathy closed her eyes, causing Theo to tremble. Could Kathy be dead? That was how people died in movies, tidily, at the end of a sentence. Kathy's eyes flickered open.

"Somebody's got to take care of Mommy," the child whispered.

Theo couldn't speak. She nodded and held Kathy's hand. The little girl closed her eyes. Theo sat on the bed, holding the swollen little hand, trying to match her breaths with Kathy's, trying to imagine God's car.

As soon as Theo had left the room, Becky sent Sally Beth to find Matt. No use convincing Mariela her dream was not a sin unless they could convince Matt. Sally Beth set off, breathing hard. She was forced to rest a few times in the hall. She felt tired but she felt no pain. Now she knew it was true. As she had discovered that morning on the sun porch, she could outrun the pain. Now she knew the pain would not return. The sun had shone through her, destroying the cancer better than the doctor's radiation. The breeze blowing through her had blown the cancer away. She was free.

"Get back to your room, Sally Beth!" The head nurse was walking down the hall, shaking her head. "Immediately!"

"OK, Theresa, everything's under control."

Passing the Playroom Sally Beth saw Matt comforting a woman. He held her, they broke apart, she wept into her hands, he held her again. Sally Beth went closer to get a look at the woman's face. "Not Barbara, not little Barbara!" Sally Beth said, much louder than she had intended. "Shit!"

Matt and the woman turned to her. Sorrow was etched across Matt's face. Sally Beth embraced the woman. "At least she's free of the pain," Sally Beth said. "We were shellacking bookends together a couple days ago. She was one tough kid."

"She wasn't supposed to die, they didn't tell us she would die. My husband wouldn't have gone to work if we had known."

"It's better this way," Sally Beth said crisply. She felt the warmth of the sun. "You wouldn't want her waiting around, in that room at the end of the hall, waiting, going slowly—"

"For God's sake, Sally Beth," Matt cried. "Please, Mrs. Moore, let me take you to Dr. Brewer's office. They'll have your husband go there directly."

"For God's sake," Sally Beth said each word slowly, "she doesn't need a shrink." Sally Beth shook her head. "You know that, Matt." Sally Beth touched the rosary clutched in Mrs. Moore's hand. "Barbara's with God," she said. "She has seen the face of Jesus. She's not sick anymore. She's out of all this."

The woman reached up and embraced Sally Beth. They held each other for several minutes. Then she turned to Matt. "I must sit beside my daughter. Will they let me stay in the room until the men come for Barbara? With the door closed?"

For an instant Sally Beth was the girl in the room behind the closed door. She was the mother too. "She's still your daughter. Death hasn't changed that."

"You bring a child into the world but you never expect to see her out."

Their plan seemed more important than ever. Sally Beth mustered her lagging energies and said to Matt, "We need you down the hall. You don't mind, Mrs. Moore?"

"No. I am going to Barbara. Thank you, Sally Beth."

"I'll be down in a few minutes," Matt said. When he was alone he ran his hands through his hair distractedly. "Who the hell is the villain?"

Reeling, the smell of Mrs. Moore's perfume still

on his hands and shirt, Matt hid out in a supply closet. At least the kids don't have our sense of permanence, death as a wipeout. Death to Sally Beth is today, now. As he consoled himself Matt scrubbed his hands and forearms with alcohol. Goddamn cancer, abscess of the soul. He glanced at his own firm muscles. Who's today's villain? Who's tomorrow's victim?

Mariela supervised Dr. Reynolds removing the tubes. "I can't believe they're out," she said. Clearly it was a sign. By removing the tubes Reynolds was saying she should go ahead, move to the next rung on the ladder. "From three tubes to zero in two minutes." She touched the doctor's arm. "You have no idea how good I feel. I won't need any blood hung tonight." She gazed at his impassive face and changed to a babyish voice. "Ma says I have good color today, my lips especially." She looked over at Becky. "You docs sure know what you're doing."

"I suppose you can go without blood tonight." He consulted Mariela's chart at the foot of her bed. He flipped through the top few pages. "You had two units last night, and platelets. And with the antibiotics—" He looked at her. "You'll be all right for the night." He collected his equipment and left.

"Thank you," Mariela called. "I always wanted to be an actress, Becky. Before, I was too fat. They say the camera adds about ten pounds. Now maybe I can."

"You sure gave a dynamite performance with

Reynolds. Now a little practice in the love-scene department—"

"Tell me honestly, do you think it's a sin, Becky?"

"Well, if it is, you'll have a lot of company in hell," Becky told her.

"Matt said he cared about me? It was his idea?"

Becky stared at her for a moment. "Of course. It was all his idea."

"Tell me exactly what he said."

"Well, what did Sally Beth tell you?" Becky wished Sally Beth would come back to help her out.

"Just that Matt confessed how he felt about me and Sally Beth offered her room, and he was so grateful to her."

"Matt said he had a *thing for you*; he should have stopped working with me last week but he had to see you." Becky was gaining confidence. The story was building inside her. "He asked me if you had a boyfriend, a steady, and I told him you had a few guys, but none serious. Then he said he could get serious but he'd wait till you were home, and he'd make his move."

Mariela hid her face and Becky knew from her lighthearted laugh that what they were doing was right. "One thing, Mariela, Matt's due to give me therapy, so don't say a word, not a look, nothing! He might back out. He's very shy."

"I'll go down to Sally Beth's room. I won't see him until tonight."

"That's even better." Becky waved her out of the

room. Sally Beth could sell ice to Eskimos. Maybe that was their ace. With Mariela all set, how could Matt refuse?

"It wasn't Kathy, it was little Barbara." Sally Beth hovered close to Becky's bed.

Becky opened her eyes and nodded. "You really did a number on Mariela! What if Matt says no?"

"What did you want me to say, we worked out a plan so you won't die a virgin?"

Becky cringed. "You made your point. Where the hell is Matt?"

"He's with Barbara's mother. He'll be down in a minute." Sally Beth's face darkened. "I never talked to one of the mothers after. It's a bummer."

"Don't tell me about it. I have enough on my mind."

"Matt should be a pushover. He looks mushy and thoroughly wiped out. It's a good time to get him. I'm going to take a nap, I feel like I've been hanging by my thumbs." Sally Beth slumped forward. "If I can only hold on so they don't hang blood tonight— 'cause if they do, Mariela will be a virgin in the morning."

"You do look sort of gray."

"Watching Barbara's mother, I kept wondering if my mother would carry on." Sally Beth picked up the mirror from Becky's nightstand. "I do look like what my grandma used to call two cents' worth of God-awful."

Theo walked into the room and burst into tears. "Not you too!" Becky said. "Come here, Theo."

Theo took Sally Beth's place on the bed and wept into Becky's arms. Becky spoke to Sally Beth over her twin's sobs. "Put on some lipstick. There's make-up in my drawer. They won't do a blood test this late in the day if you look halfway alive."

"Good thing we have Annie on tonight. She never checks us. Lazy cow!"

Theo's sobs tapered off. What strength it took for Sally Beth to be so tough, to harden her terrors into attack. The cancer destroyed more than her blood. Theo wondered what she had been like before she was diagnosed.

She hugged Sally Beth. "I love you."

Sally Beth grimaced. "What's that all about?"

Becky waved her hand. "Both of you split before Matt comes. And keep Mariela under wraps. Theo, stop sniveling!"

"I'll hide in the john. He won't see me," Theo said. "Thanks for letting me have a part."

"Thanks for wanting one," Becky said. Each held the other's glance for a moment. "Now quick, into the john, Theo!"

"I won't say a word." Theo barely had time to slip into the bathroom before Matt appeared in the doorway.

"Now what's your problem, Becky?" Theo opened the bathroom door a crack.

"I heard about little Barbara. Lousy!"

Matt sat on the foot of Becky's bed and began to flex her foot. "Now push against my hand—"

"That's not why I called you," Becky said softly. She couldn't look directly at Matt. "Barbara and Kathy—" she began.

"Don't think about them, sugar. There are no signs of malignant cells anywhere in your body. Your lungs are clear."

"Mariela's slipping."

"We mustn't give up hope."

"She's got one wish, Matt."

"This kind of talk is no good. You concentrate on getting well, going back to your family and friends. Your workouts have made the difference. Your leg muscles are stronger every day."

Becky reached for Matt's hand. "She doesn't want to die a virgin. Please, Matt, we need you, you're not like the rest of the staff."

"Just what is it you want me to do?"

"Sleep with Mariela."

Matt stared unblinking at Becky.

Becky glanced at the partially open bathroom door. Theo's presence gave Becky the strength to continue. "Don't go virtuous, priggish on me, Matt. We are lucky we can do something for Mariela."

"It's impossible," Matt insisted.

Theo was amazed at Becky's calm. She talked as though she were holding all the cards. This was a different game. A game of survival against all defeats. A vital game that Theo had not needed to learn.

[237]

"She forced herself to eat so they would take out the tubes. She got up and walked. So she could switch rooms with Sally Beth. You know what that must have cost her."

Matt glanced at Mariela's empty bed. "What made her think that I—"

"She has such a crush on you," Becky said simply. "It's all she wants."

"She's not going to leave—" Matt recovered himself. "There's no way."

"There is. After night meds, Sally Beth will slip in here and Mariela will go down there, probably about ten-thirty when the nurses are changing shifts."

"It's not possible. If the staff found out. If her parents found out!" Matt rubbed his palm over his face. "It's not something you do on command." Even as he said the words he felt foolish, sanctimonious. The nice rules were all blown to hell in this place, where the eyes of the youngest children held the knowledge of acute suffering one moment and gleeful merriment the next.

He was so often shattered by his own helplessness. Becky's gentle smile clarified his dilemma. What the girls were asking was that he respond to Mariela's need. If he admitted their human connection, each to the other, he would spend this night with Mariela. It required no medical wizardry, no miracle. He did have the human warmth Mariela needed. It was more necessary to her now than all the drugs and transfusions.

"You are right," Matt said softly. "Wish I had thought of it myself." He squeezed Becky's hand. "I'll be there. Ten-thirty."

After he left Becky picked up a mirror and studied her reflection. The dread will never disappear like water down a basin drain. Always this uncertainty, but along the way a sense of healing, a temporary victory when time seems like a blessing instead of a curse. Tonight will be a victory for all of us, Becky thought.

"Come out, Theo, stop hiding behind the door," Becky called, her voice resonant and vital.

Theo approached Becky's bed. "I never thought he would go through with it," she whispered. "I thought it was somewhere between a joke and a game."

Becky was touched by her twin's confusion. It was so hard for Theo to acknowledge their differences, especially now that they were no longer in the same place.

Theo shook her head. "You knew Matt would do it."

Becky nodded.

Theo was still for a moment. Slowly she drew back the sheet that covered Becky's braced leg. She lifted the gauze and stared at the wound, sat down next to it on the bed and bent even closer to it. Her hands were cold against Becky's skin. After several minutes Theo looked up at her sister. Her head was inches away from the wound, her mouth was set firmly.

"I'm sorry I never looked at it before. The stitches are like a zipper track."

"Look at what they use to suture it—*black thread*. I had thought it would be something more exotic." Becky put her hand on top of Theo's.

"They're like basting stitches. Is Titelbaum sure it will hold?" Theo traced the stitches with her fingertip.

"You're right, they are like basting stitches. Titelbaum takes them out when the wound's healed."

Theo mimed sewing the wound closed. "If only we could sew up everything as neatly as Titelbaum did your leg." Very gently she replaced the gauze pad over the wound. "You have no idea how often I've prayed we could stay together on the same side of the door. Since you were diagnosed I've been so lonely."

Becky smoothed the adhesive strip over the bandage. "But we can listen for each other, Theo. We can talk to each other through the door."

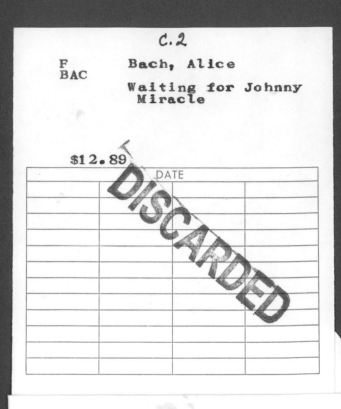